HELEN R. MYERS

Someone to Watch over Me

Silhouette Romance

Published by Silhouette Books New York

America's Publisher of Contemporary Romance

For my lovely stepdaughters—
Julie, Robyn, Bobbie and Tammy—
who think it's fun to see the family name in print

SILHOUETTE BOOKS
300 E. 42nd St., New York, N.Y. 10017

Copyright © 1989 by Helen R. Myers

ISBN: 0-373-08643-1

First Silhouette Books printing April 1989

HELEN R. MYERS

lives on a sixty-five-acre ranch deep in the piney woods of east Texas with her husband, Robert, and a constantly expanding menagerie. She lists her interests as everything that doesn't have to do with a needle and thread. When she and Robert aren't working on the house they've built together she likes to read, garden and, of course, outfish her husband.

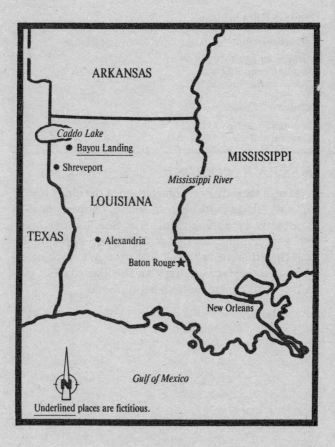

ARKANSAS

Caddo Lake
● Bayou Landing

● Shreveport

MISSISSIPPI

Mississippi River

LOUISIANA

TEXAS

● Alexandria

Baton Rouge ★

New Orleans

Gulf of Mexico

Underlined places are fictitious.

Chapter One

She noticed the place the moment the bus pulled into the dingy little gas-station depot. It would have been impossible not to: in the dark it appeared to be the only other business in the town that the driver had identified as Bayou Landing, Louisiana. But she knew it would do the moment she realized the shamrock-green neon sign advertised more than a motel and café. O'Neal's was first and foremost a lounge. The number of cars and pickups parked out front verified that. To her it was as welcoming a sight as a port would be to a seaman caught in a storm. And so was the Help Wanted sign stuck in one of the front windows.

The building wasn't fancy: the walls were formed of smooth stone; light and music were attractively contained by the louvered shutters on its tall windows; and across the breezeway through the plate-glass windows she could see that vinyl, Formica and chrome were still the standard decorating scheme for a roadside café. But it was clean, business looked brisk—and there *was* that sign in the window. More than anything else, it was that which convinced her to slip her purse strap over her shoulder and get off the bus.

Heat and the stench of gas fumes purged by the idling engine attacked her senses simultaneously, causing her a momentary wave of nausea. She willed it away and signaled to the driver, who'd completed his business with the station attendant and was returning to the bus.

"I'd like to have my bag, please."

As she expected, he looked confused. "But you just got on in Shreveport; your ticket's paid to Little Rock."

"I've changed my mind," she replied, her voice almost drowned out by the low rumble of the engine.

Without further comment he unlocked the baggage compartment, and without hesitation reached for the battered brown suitcase inside—no impressive reflection of his memory since she was one of only three passengers. Setting it at her feet, he turned back to secure the door.

"Next bus out of here will be tomorrow night."

Reaching for the case, she smiled wryly. She could appreciate his thinking she was crazy; a young woman traveling alone didn't usually get off a bus at this hour of the night in the middle of nowhere. But she was relying on her instincts these days, and they were telling her that she could be safe here.

"Thanks," she murmured. "But I'm not planning on needing it."

The driver shrugged, his duty done, and climbed aboard the bus. A moment later, following the surging sound of released air brakes and that of grinding gears, the silver-and-red behemoth crawled past her, turned back onto the single-lane highway and was soon nothing more than two red eyes surrounded by darkness. Before she could step out of the cloud of foul-smelling smoke the bus left behind, the rumble of its powerful engine was replaced by the more delicate chorus of crickets and tree frogs.

Just inside the open door of the station an elderly black man sat in a cane rocker. Its subtle creaking added a pleasant accompaniment to the night sounds. He was long-limbed and so skinny his overalls lay almost flat against the chair. His T-shirt was a startling white against his ebony skin and made his short hair seem more like a collection of dust on a vacuum-cleaner filter than the near white it was. His face was serene, deeply lined, and dominated by clear brown eyes and a wide, flat-lipped mouth. When she stepped through the doorway, he broke into a wide smile that exposed a collection of brilliant white-and-gold teeth. It took no effort at all to smile back.

"Come in, missy. Come in an' rest a spell," he said, beckoning her closer with a bony hand. "Ol' Jesse don't mind watching over one of the Lord's lost sheep. No sir. Got a cool fan an' a comfortable chair. Come in."

There was also, she noticed, a double-barreled shotgun leaning against the wall within reaching distance, inclining her to believe that old Jesse might also trust that the meek shall inherit the earth, but he wasn't taking any chances.

"Thanks, Jesse," she murmured, setting her case down beside the old armchair he indicated. If he'd already decided she was a lost sheep, she must look worse than she imagined. "What I'd really like is to use your washroom."

As she spoke she glanced around, taking in the chipped paint walls and the bare light-bulb dangling from the ceiling. It wasn't reassuring, and she hoped she wasn't about to be given directions to some facilities out back, but the old man simply pointed to a door at the far side of the room.

"Mind you be careful of Missus an' the family," he added. "They be set in for the night."

Wondering who "Missus" was and what she was going to think about sharing her accommodations, she went to find out. The bathroom was no bigger than a closet and painted the same bland beige as the rest of the building. It smelled of disinfectant and Kitty Litter. Tucked beneath a dripping faucet and washbasin was a box containing the reason why. A well-fed calico cat, curled around five tiny bundles of equally multicolored fur, gave her a soft mew of inquiry.

"Hello, Missus," she whispered, stooping to get a closer look and barely refraining from offering the mother cat a scratch behind the ear. "Sorry for the intrusion. I only want to wash up and then I'll be out of your way. Fair enough?"

She received what she could only assume was a sound of acceptance and straightened to study her reflection in the dime-store mirror hanging over the sink. It was enough to make her groan in despair.

No, she wasn't ready to walk into O'Neal's. Her hair needed a vigorous brushing, there was a smudge of dust on her cheek—probably gotten while she rested her head against the bus window—and she was too pale. Without a touch of lipstick or blush, her dark eyes swallowed her face and made her seem younger than her twenty-three years. She certainly didn't need that strike against her, and unzipping her purse, she took out the small container of soap she always carried, and went to work.

A short time later she shook her head, and her shiny mane of black hair, cut in a long shag, settled to curl naturally around her face. Then she stepped back to scrutinize the results. Better, she decided, noting that the touch of rose on her cheeks and lips helped delineate those features. Yet by no means did she see the beauty others credited her with; she only saw a too-small mouth, a nose that could have been a smidgen longer to suggest character, and a chin too sharp to fit her otherwise delicately contoured face. Lately she'd been happy to underplay her looks, but now she couldn't afford to take any chances.

She wasn't as satisfied when she dropped her gaze to her white shirt and jeans. They didn't look as bad as they felt; sticky and damp with perspiration because the air conditioner on the bus had malfunctioned, they only looked a bit wrinkled. They would have to do. She'd packed in a hurry and didn't doubt that whatever was in her suitcase looked in much the same condition. However, she *did* momentarily finger the second button on her shirt. It might distract attention from her clothes—but it could also *attract* trouble. And wasn't she in enough of that already?

With a faint sigh she reached for her purse, and out of the corner of her eye caught the cat watching her with apparent interest. "Don't look at me that way," she mumbled. "At least I don't have your problem."

Jesse was still in his chair rocking and gazing outside, oblivious to the moths circling about the light overhead, and thinking who knew what. His apparent serenity over what life had yielded him reminded her of her aunt and uncle, and of happier times—memories that left her with a bittersweet ache.

She cleared her throat. "Bayou Landing... Does that mean we're near Caddo Lake?"

"It's right behind O'Neal's," Jesse said, nodding. Then he turned to look at her and his eyes lit with appreciation. "My, don't you look nice. Course you don't need all that rouge to look pretty. How come you got off that bus without knowing where you was at?"

"Inspiration." At his frown, she tilted her head toward the lounge. "I saw that sign in the window. I need a job."

"Well, Mr. Dane treats his people real fine. I didn't expect that sign would stay up for more than a day or two."

"Really? In that case maybe I'd better get on over there. Do you think I could leave my suitcase here? How long do you stay open?"

"Till I gets tired of staying awake." He slapped at his knee, tickled at his own wit. "Sure, you leave it. I'll be here. About closing time's when somebody over there remembers they's almost out of gas. It'll cost you, though."

Didn't everything? When was she going to learn? "How much?"

"Your name."

Tension seeped out of her as quickly as it had come. She stepped out into the night and glanced up at the stars, remembering a time when her chief preoccupation had been wondering whether God had created more of them than fireflies.

"Stevi," she said simply.

He never broke the rhythm of his rocking, although she was sure he was waiting for more. When it didn't come, he nodded and calmly refolded his hands across his flat belly. ''Well, welcome to Bayou Landing, Stevi. I hope you find whatever it is you're looking for.''

Murmuring her thanks, she left Jesse to return to his own thoughts. Her tennis shoes barely made a sound on the packed clay ground, and before she got very far from the minimal relief of his oscillating fan, heat and humidity quickly wrapped themselves around her again. The air felt thick enough to cut with a butter knife, she thought, feeling a droplet of sweat slip down between her breasts, and the only productive thing about it was the size of the mosquitoes it spawned. She killed one the size of a cotton ball before it could bite her, then pulled out a tissue from her purse and dabbed it to her throat and chest.

Stepping inside the lounge, she experienced an instant impulse to sigh with relief, but it was only partially due to the air-conditioning. It was the lounge itself; it was perfect. She'd been concerned that her instincts might be off—that it was simply a redneck bar with pool tables and a jukebox. It wasn't.

Mellow jazz flowed around her, and candles flickered on the tables and along the bar, illuminating an otherwise dark-paneled room. All the booths that lined two walls were occupied and about a third of the tables. On the postage-stamp-size dance floor, one lone couple swayed together, blissfully unaware of onlookers, and in the far corner was a piano—a baby grand, no less.

As she glanced around, she felt attention swing her way. Before she could brush the last droplets of moisture from between her breasts, conversation around the bar dwindled noticeably. Unperturbed, she tucked the tissue into her jeans pocket. Over the past few years she'd learned to get used to being stared at, and to acquire a talent for ignoring it. At the moment the only person's attention she was interested in was the bartender's, though he looked like a biker with his long, kinky hair pulled back into a ponytail and his full beard. But as she met his open stare she saw he had eyes like Bambi and decided he might not be too bad to deal with, after all.

"Evening," he said as she stepped up to the bar. "What'll it be?"

"A job."

He'd been reaching for a cocktail napkin, and hearing her reply, missed. "Oh."

"Aren't you O'Neal?" Somehow the name fit him; he was easily six six, his hands all palms—reminding her of bear paws—and she doubted there were many women who had arms long enough to reach completely around his chest.

"Naw. That was the original owner. He died about three years ago. They call me Sweet, only because I outgrew Timothy by the time I was nine and I can't abide Oliver. Anyway, you want to talk to Dane. Dane Randolph. See that door over there marked Office? Just knock and go on in."

Stevi thanked him and started circling the bar. So this "Mr. Dane" Jesse had mentioned was a Randolph not an O'Neal, she mused, and obviously well liked. He was probably an elderly man who'd once dreamed of having his own bistro in New Orleans but had had to settle here. It would take a cockeyed optimist to make a success of something like this, way out in the middle of nowhere. She hoped he would find a soft spot in his heart for her. She wouldn't be able to promise him longevity, but while she was here she would work hard at whatever task he gave her.

Her knock on the door was immediately answered by a gruff "Yeah?" and taking a deep breath, she entered.

"Sweet, where the hell's Henri? Does he think that piano's going to play itself? And what are we doing with all these maraschino cherries? This invoice says—"

"Mr. Randolph? Excuse me, but I'm not Sweet."

That, Dane Randolph thought as he shot a quick look over his shoulder and realized his error, was debatable.

Stevi took in the endless length of blue jeans-clad legs crossed negligently and resting on the edge of the desk, the windblown brown hair that curled around the collar of a black safari shirt, the rakish mustache and sudden, equally rakish smile—and reached for the door she'd just closed.

"Wait a minute."

"Maybe I'd better—"

"You wanted to see me."

No, she wanted to see the nice, elderly man she'd envisioned—not this tall, lanky *cowboy* who looked as if he could charm a rattlesnake out of its rattles. She didn't need to be charmed; she had enough problems. *But you need a job,* she reminded herself.

Sighing, she released the doorknob and turned back into the room, closing both hands in a stranglehold around the strap of her purse. "I saw the Help Wanted sign in the window."

Following some inexplicable instinct, Dane had risen the moment he saw her reaching for the door; now, sensing she still might bolt, he followed yet another and forced himself to wait. "You want to be a cocktail waitress?"

"Fine."

"Pardon?" His laugh was brief, a little confused.

"I didn't know what the job was for, but that's fine. I'll take it . . . I mean, if you'll let me."

His dark brown eyes twinkled suspiciously as he gestured to the chair facing his desk. "Why don't you come sit down. And relax."

It had been weeks since she'd felt anything close to relaxed, and she was beginning to wonder if she would ever feel that way again. It certainly wasn't going to happen if she had to spend much time around *him*, she thought, reluctantly taking the seat he'd indicated. There was one other man who made it impossible for her to maintain a detached air—but never in this way; not in this safe yet unsafe way.

"Why don't we start over," he said, tossing the invoice for the cherries on top of the stack of other bills and shoving them all to the side of his desk. "You obviously know who I am. And you are . . . ?"

"Stevi."

"Just Stevi?" Winged brows lifted in amusement. "And here I thought it was only people in show business who went by a single name."

"Stevi James," she said quickly. "Your bartender told me who you were, and that I needed to talk to you about the job. I can work any shift and I don't mind long hours."

He let his gaze drift over her. Her jet-black hair was glossy like the semiprecious stone, her olive skin smooth and unlined. Her eyes fascinated him; were they really indigo blue or was it the lighting that created those mysterious shadows?

"Obviously you haven't been in the business long."

She dropped her own gaze to the purse in her lap. "Mr. Randolph, the truth is—"

"Dane."

She glanced up and saw, incredibly, that he already knew what she was going to tell him—*and* that he liked looking at her. Maybe the one would offset the other. "I've never actually done any type of waitressing before, but I'm a fast learner and I have a good memory. I'm also good with figures," she added, remembering she hadn't yet been twenty when she'd taken over running the household for her aunt.

"You forgot persistent," he murmured, wondering why there wasn't someone in her life to save her from having to do this. A career was one thing, but being a cocktail waitress was a job, pure and simple, and often a grueling one. He dropped his gaze to her long-fingered hands—ringless hands—then reminded himself that the absence of rings meant little these days. Maybe there was a man and he couldn't make ends meet; the economic crunch was hurting a lot of people. Or maybe he was simply a louse. "Why don't you tell me something about yourself," he coaxed, finding himself wanting to know the answers more than he would have cared to admit.

"Do I have to fill out a job application to wait on tables?"

"What you have to do is convince me you want the job," he replied, a hint of steel entering his own voice.

Want? She almost laughed. What she wanted was to wake up and discover that the past six weeks had only been a bad dream. She wanted to go to sleep at night and know for once that she wouldn't be waking up a few hours later feverish and pressing her hand to her mouth to hold back a scream. Wanting had nothing to do with why she was sitting here.

"I *need* the job."

"Money problems?"

"Survival problems."

"Married?"

"No."

"Children?"

"I told you I'm not married."

He ran a finger over his mustache to hide a smile. "How old are you?"

"Twenty-four. Well, next month."

Dane sat back in his chair to once again lift his booted feet up onto the desk, then folded his hands across his flat belly. She intrigued him. When was the last time he'd met a woman who was already counting her next birthday, had traditional beliefs about kids and marriage, and yet who looked like the kind of woman modeling agencies used for lingerie ads? She was too good to be true, and that was probably why she was as tight-lipped as a clam about herself. She was hiding something. Under different circumstances he would have wanted to make sure he knew what it was before he hired her; he wasn't much for surprises. But Marge and Penny had already threatened mutiny if they were left to handle the weekend crowd on their own. He couldn't bring in Jolene until next week because he still needed her in the café, and— No, the truth of the matter was he didn't want this mystery lady walking out of his office without being certain she would be back.

"Okay," he murmured, before he could call himself several kinds of crazy. "We'll give it a shot. Provided you pass muster, that is."

"Excuse me?"

"We're a pretty tight group here. I've known Sweet for almost fifteen years, my waitresses have been here since I've owned the place. Even Henri, when he isn't chasing stardom and leaving me high and dry, is like family.''

''The man who's supposed to relieve the stereo,'' she murmured dryly, catching on.

''Exactly.'' Dane's smile was a quick flash of white against his dark tan and darker mustache. ''Think you can handle it?''

She didn't have much choice, did she? However, she would have been comfortable if she didn't have the feeling he was asking her a double-edged question.

''Come on,'' he said before she could answer. He rose and came around to her side of the desk.

He wasn't as tall as Sweet, but as Stevi stood up she realized he was still over six feet and towered over her own five-foot-five. Close up she discovered there were fine lines to accompany the deeper ones on his long, narrow face, which suggested he either smiled a lot or spent most of his time outdoors. Still, it was an attractive face full of strength and character. His forehead and chin were square, his nose long and narrow, his mouth wide and firm. She guessed him to be in his mid- to late thirties and decided that sun and laughter had marked him kindly. But looking into his dark brown eyes she saw no hint of laughter now; only the attraction of a man for a woman, and many questions.

Tearing her gaze from his, she led the way to the door and almost jumped when his arm brushed against her as he took hold of the doorknob. Or was it because his warm breath touched her hair near her ear? Never was she more grateful for the company of strangers than when they stepped into the lounge.

Henri Chennault was back at the piano stirring up his audience with a frenzied medley of Jerry Lee Lewis songs. Small and fragile-boned with fine strawberry-blond hair, he made Stevi think of a sparrow who had inadvertently landed on a hot electrical wire. As he bounced spasmodically in time to the music, she felt Dane take her arm.

"He's good," she said, letting him lead her toward the far side of the bar where several stools were available.

"He's depressed."

Taking the corner stool, she gave him a doubtful look. "Did you say—"

"Depressed." Dane slid onto the stool beside hers. "Our Henri is something of a rare bird, isn't that right, Sweet?" he murmured to the bartender, who joined them.

"He's nuts," the big man corrected, placing a cocktail napkin before each of them. "When he's happy he won't play anything but the blues. When he's in the dumps..." He hooked his thumb over his shoulder indicating the show going on and gave Stevi a pained look. "If you ask me, somebody dropped him when he was a baby. I've told Dane next time he takes off on us we should sell that piano to a toothpick factory, extend the dance floor, and invest in one of those disc players. But the boss here is a nicer guy than I am."

"I'm not sure Stevi would agree with you," Dane said, enjoying the way her softly bowed mouth twitched at Sweet's unintentional humor.

Startled, she whipped her head around. "I don't think you're—" The rest of her words were lost somewhere between her brain and her mouth, short-circuited out of existence by the stronger current created when she felt Dane's eyes searching hers.

"You don't?"

"No."

"Thank you. I might have taken up playing a little Jerry Lee myself if you did. If I could play, that is."

Stop it, her eyes telegraphed to his. *This isn't what I want.*

What do you want?

Sweet coughed discreetly and asked them what they would like to drink. Stevi shot him a grateful look.

Still, it took her a moment to answer. She hadn't eaten since morning and worried that wine would go straight to her head. Finally, she ordered a Bloody Mary, considering its at least minimal nutritional value.

Dane ordered a beer and told his friend he was thinking about offering Stevi the job. "By the way, did you two introduce yourselves before?"

"Halfway," Stevi admitted. When Sweet placed her drink before her, she extended her hand and gave him her name.

"Welcome aboard."

"I think I'm jealous," Dane murmured. "That's more than I got."

Stevi ignored him and told Sweet, "He hasn't hired me yet."

"He will." Sweet brought Dane his beer. "You want me to send over the girls?"

"Good idea. We'll save Henri for later and when he's not so—wound."

Marge and Penny proved to be even more enthusiastic than Sweet at the news of Stevi's joining the staff, and generously dismissed her warning about her lack of experience.

"You don't need experience with this job," Marge drawled. "You need *endurance.*" She was a plump woman in her early forties, whom Stevi saw as a cross between a kindergarten teacher and a drill instructor.

In comparison, Penny was no less warm but far more quiet. Tall, with a girlish gawkiness despite the fact that she had to be in her late thirties, she stood to one side, clutching her tray to her modest breasts. When it came time for her to speak to Stevi, she simply rushed forward, gave her a quick hug, then went back to her tables.

"You'll get used to Penny," Marge assured her. "She's our resident flower child."

But when Marge also left, it was Dane who noticed Stevi blinking furiously, and who leaned closer to voice his concern. Not wanting him to see the tears burning in her eyes, she turned her head away for a moment until she had herself back under control.

"Excuse me. I've had a long day and I guess I'm more tired than I realized."

"Of course," Dane murmured, accepting that although he wasn't sure he believed it. Resisting the strong urge to embrace her himself, he quickly ran through her schedule and her salary, which would naturally be higher when her tips were included. "Is that satisfactory?"

"Yes. Fine." She slid off the stool. "Thank you, Mr. Randolph."

"Dane."

"Dane," she repeated, focusing on the dark thatch of hair exposed by the open collar of his shirt. "Then I'll see you tomorrow."

As she started to move away he caught her arm, but feeling her immediate stiffening, he quickly released her. "Easy, honey. I only wanted to ask where you live," he said quietly.

"Nowhere, yet."

"Pardon?"

She glanced at Sweet, who made no pretense of hiding his own curiosity, then back at Dane. "I—um—I just got off a bus. Getting a job was my first priority."

The silence that followed seemed to last an eternity. Stevi didn't know why everyone in the room seemed unaware of the little drama being played out between them; but conversations continued along the bar, and Henri mellowed out to playing Gershwin.

Finally, although it could only have been seconds later, Dane reached across the bar and without breaking eye contact with her, held out his hand to Sweet. Obviously he knew what Dane wanted because he went straight to the cash register and returned to place something in his hand.

Dane tossed it to Stevi. It was a key. "There's a duplex out back," he explained. "The left side is vacant."

"Who's in the right?"

"Me."

Her mouth twisting into a bitter smile, Stevi tossed the key back to him. "Thanks, but no thanks. I'm only looking for a job, not a roommate."

"Wait until you're asked," he muttered, tossing the key back again.

Haven't you?

So I'm human. "Look, you need a good night's sleep. The locks are solid. Take it."

What was she getting herself into? she wondered, closing her fingers around the key and feeling it bite into her flesh. These were nice people. He was a decent man. One put down roots with people like this. She couldn't afford to do that—not to them, not to herself. But she was so tired.

"Okay. Thanks," she murmured, and whispering good-night, she quickly turned on her heel and left.

When the front door closed behind her, Dane swiveled back toward the bar only to find Sweet eyeing him speculatively.

"Kinda strange lady," the giant mused.

Dane rotated his beer between his hands.

"Pretty, though."

Still ignoring Sweet, Dane drank the remaining beer and then indicated he wanted a refill.

Sweet returned in a moment and placed the fresh beer before him. "Sad eyes."

"Yeah," Dane murmured. "I noticed."

Chapter Two

When she first opened her eyes the next morning, Stevi felt a moment or two of disorientation. Then she recognized the white, carved egrets on the bureau top she'd admired last night. Bayou Landing... O'Neal's... Dane Randolph... It all came back in a rush.

She raised herself up on her elbows and glanced around the room. Except for the few pieces of artwork—the egrets, an owl on a shelf over the doorway and a pair of mallards on the wall beside the bed—the room could have been one in the motel. The king-size bed that she'd had to make up with sheets she found in a closet last night was comfortable enough, the blue-and-green color scheme of the walls and carpet were pleasant, but the room lacked the accessories and knickknacks it took to make a house a home. Of course Dane Randolph had explained that the place was vacant, hadn't he? But then whom did the wood carvings belong to? Though she was no expert, she thought they were good; surely they hadn't been left behind by the previous resident? Maybe they belonged to her new employer. Maybe he found it relaxing to occupy himself in this kind of hobby in his spare time. Her thoughts drifted back to last night and she remembered his hands—their strength and the slight roughness of his callused skin; the way his long fingers had closed around her arm, causing a faint tingling sensation to race down her spine.

With an abrupt, dismissive shake of her head, she tossed back the sheet and pushed herself out of bed. If that was the way her mind was going to work, she would do well to remind herself of her predicament. For everyone's sake, the less interested—not to mention the less involved—she became with the people she met, the better. Strangers were easier to walk away from than friends, and although last night it had seemed that she could settle and be happy here, only time would tell.

After a refreshing shower, Stevi dried her hair and slipped into clean jeans and a mesh tank top in stone beige that she decided were the least wrinkled things in her suitcase. By then, her stomach was pulling from hunger and her system was sending out equally irrepressible messages that it wanted its daily dosage of caffeine. Last night's inspection of the kitchen had yielded only the knowledge that if she intended to eat, it would be down in the café, so, retrieving her wallet from her purse, she checked her finances to see how well she could satisfy either craving.

What she found wasn't encouraging. Forty-three dollars and change wasn't much of a bankroll, particularly when she still needed to find a place to live. Leaving Shreveport without her paycheck had hurt, and buying her bus ticket almost wiped out her meager savings.

There went her mouth-watering daydreams of French toast drenched with maple syrup and juicy link sausages. Coffee and a doughnut would have to do, especially since she needed to be able to afford some kind of dinner. Lunch she would have to do without.

When she let herself out the front door, she found the sun already hot and blinding. It was going to be another steamy August day. The heat made the Spanish moss draping the cypress trees appear even more gray and limp, but she loved the image it evoked: romantic, mysterious. It called to that trace of blood in her veins that was Cajun, and eased the ache of homesickness.

She was delighted to find, not far beyond the porch, one of the innumerable channels that collectively joined to make Caddo Lake. As a child in school, she'd read the Indians' version of how the lake was formed; how earth spirits, angered at a Caddo Indian chief, shook the earth violently one night during the dark of the moon. She hoped she would be around long enough to explore some of it.

Descending the stairs, she continued to inspect her new surroundings. The house, raised on stilts, was painted white with green trim, matching the sides and back of the lounge and café. It was set back and away from the two-story brick motel and given additional privacy by an eight-foot-high fence, charmingly covered with honeysuckle vines that were in their second bloom. In the shade of a group of pine trees was a picnic table and brick barbecue pit, the ground around which was well trampled, suggesting frequent use. Against the back wall of a storage shed in dire need of painting, pink wild roses did their best to improve the view.

Walking along the breezeway separating the café from the lounge, Stevi picked up the first tantalizing scents of cooking. It made the hollowness in her stomach feel more like a bottomless pit, and she tried not to remember that yesterday's menu had consisted of a vending-machine package of cookies, a greasy hamburger and the drink she'd had at the bar.

Inside the café, she found several booths and a few of the counter seats occupied. Most of the people had their noses buried in either the morning paper or their breakfasts. Everyone, that is, except the waitress who came up to take her order.

"Say—I know you."

Stevi's stomach plummeted like an elevator that had had its cables severed, but she managed to give the curly-haired blonde a polite smile. "No, I don't think so. I'd like a large coffee and a sweet roll. To go, please."

Instead of writing, the waitress pointed to her with the eraser end of her pencil. "It was last night, next door. You're the other new cocktail waitress. I'm Jolene Frazier. I'll be working there, too; next week, since they've found someone to replace me here. I'm sorry I didn't come introduce myself with the others, but I'm still a little slow with getting out my orders. For some reason, carrying a tray of cocktails intimidates me more than balancing four plates of spaghetti."

Unable to resist Jolene's twinkling green eyes and the sprinkling of freckles that dusted her nose, Stevi warmed her smile by several degrees. "Don't say that. This is going to be my first time at it, too."

"Great. We'll be misfits together. But don't let me scare you," Jolene said, pouring the coffee and wrapping the roll in wax paper. "We couldn't ask for a better boss; Dane's the best."

"So I've heard," Stevi murmured, digging out the correct change from her wallet. Then she picked up her sack. "Well, I guess I'll see you around."

"Maybe we can talk sometime during our breaks."

"Sure."

But once outside and out of sight, Stevi paused and drew her lower lip between her teeth. This was exactly what she needed to avoid. Jolene wasn't much older than she was, and she seemed nice; but along with friendship came questions—questions she couldn't afford. She'd learned the hard way how people who befriended her could get hurt.

She was back at the top of the stairs when she smelled the delicious aroma that annulled the pleasant one rising from her sack. It drifted through the screen door and windows of Dane Randolph's place and had her urgently digging into her pocket for her key. She didn't need to be talking to him, either—at least not before she *had* to. But before she could put the key in the lock, he was poking his head around the screen door.

"Morning! I thought I saw you coming up the stairs. Come on over and join me."

"No, really, I—" She barely got that far before he disappeared back into his place. "Great," she muttered under her breath. Now how was she going to get herself out of this? If she made believe she hadn't heard him, he would probably come looking for her in a minute. And he *was* her boss; it wouldn't be wise to offend him before she even started her new job.

Reluctantly she began crossing the deck. She would eat her food quickly, she decided, then make some kind of excuse and leave.

The moment she stepped into his kitchen, she found herself under the intent scrutiny of not one but two pairs of eyes, and though Dane's expression smoothly eased into a welcoming smile, the black German shepherd lying at his feet continued to stare. When she took another hesitant step, it raised its head and uttered a low growl.

"Quiet," Dane grumbled, his voice nearly as deep as the dog's. "Can't you tell a friend when you see one?" As if it understood, the shepherd wagged its tail once before dropping its head back onto its front paws, while Dane gestured with a spatula toward the cozy booth built in by the double windows. "Have a seat. This is almost ready."

"That's okay, I have my own." She slid into the side without the place setting and began to remove the coffee and roll from the bag. The tantalizing smell wafting around her with the help of a ceiling fan was making her mouth water, and she was afraid that if she didn't eat something soon, her stomach was going to embarrass her.

"Oh, yeah? What did you get?" Dane came over and inspected her intended meal, but a moment later he scowled and snatched up both items.

Stevi watched openmouthed as he tossed the sweet roll to the dog, who devoured it in one impossible gulp, and poured her coffee into the sink. "Hey! That was my breakfast!"

"This will taste better than drinking it out of Styrofoam," he replied, pouring fresh coffee from a pot into a sturdy mug. He brought it over and set it before her.

"Breakfast will be ready in a minute. Do you like your eggs scrambled or over easy?"

"I *like* sweet rolls, and if *taste* was the issue you could have just as easily poured my own coffee into that mug."

His grin was unapologetic. "Drink your coffee. Are you always this feisty in the morning?"

She wrapped her hands around the mug to keep them from trembling and continued her glare of resentment. "Are you always this bossy?"

"Only when I run across someone who looks like they need a good meal in them but they're too proud to admit it. Eggs?"

Her annoyance gave way to resignation. "Scrambled—please." There was no sense arguing with him when he was right. It had been a long time since her appetite was what it used to be, and she *was* proud. The aunt and uncle who'd raised her had been hardworking people, religious people. From them she had learned to take pleasure in making her own way in the world and to leave charity for those who were incapable of helping themselves. It wasn't something she could easily shut off like tap water.

She took an eager but careful sip of her steaming coffee. It was rich, though it lacked the strong chickory flavor she'd been raised on. She wasn't surprised; she'd already decided that Dane Randolph wasn't a native. By his looks and a certain inflection in his drawl, she guessed he was a Texan from the far western part of the state. Texans had a unique charm for acting as if the whole world were their own backyard, and they reminded her of those longhorn cattle they were so famous for: resilient. Casting Dane an oblique look, she decided the latter term suited him particularly well.

Like her, he was wearing jeans and a tank top. His was black and it accented his lean, powerful build to the point of distraction. In the bright sunlight streaking through the windows beside her, she saw that he was tanned to a deep bronze and the long muscles along his arms and across his broad shoulders stretched easily like sinewy rawhide. The climbing temperature and ever-present humidity were raising a fine mist of sweat beneath the dusting of hair along his forearms and above the thicker mat of hair exposed by the low cut of his tank top. The effect was so disturbingly sexual that she felt her own body grow uncomfortably warm. She set down her mug and rubbed her damp palms along her thighs.

"What's the matter, coffee too hot?" he asked, bringing her plate to the table.

"A little." She avoided his probing gaze, which was easier to do once she saw what he expected her to eat. Ham, eggs, and gravy-covered biscuits were heaped upon her plate. She glanced over at the plate he put down for himself and saw it was equally laden.

"Better too much than not enough," he said, returning with silverware and a napkin for her. When he'd retrieved his own mug from the counter, he slid into his side of the booth, only to have his leg, from thigh to ankle, come up hard against hers. "Damn, sorry," he muttered, feeling her jerk away. "I've been meaning to widen this thing to fit my long legs for ages, but I keep putting it off."

Stevi didn't know which was more difficult to ignore—having his thigh pressed so intimately against hers, or looking up to find him so close she could see herself reflected in his dark eyes. Knowing she wouldn't be able to swallow a bite of food without doing something about their proximity, she squirmed in her seat and tucked her legs up into a lotus position.

"It might not be good table etiquette," she explained at his bemused look. "But at least you'll have more room."

He wasn't fooled; she hadn't withdrawn like a turtle into its shell for his benefit alone. Having him touch her, even being in the same room with him, made her tense; he'd noticed that last night. But he also knew how he intended to handle her: quietly, gently, as he would a wounded, frightened creature he might come upon in the woods.

"Nice trick," he drawled, peering under the table. "If I tried that, I'd be stuck here until Sweet showed up with a crowbar to untangle me. How're the eggs? Not too dry?"

She hadn't tasted them yet, hadn't tasted anything. She didn't know if she could get anything past the block in her throat, but she forced herself to try. To her relief and delight, the eggs were delicious and seemed to melt away the invisible barrier.

Dane chuckled softly and sliced his ham. "Well, you don't have to look that surprised. I've never poisoned anyone yet. Sweet's the one who needs a keeper. He's a terrific bartender, but if he ever offers to cook you anything—even something simple like a hamburger— run, don't walk, to the nearest exit. Once he single-handedly incapacitated an entire oil-rig crew when he took over the kitchen after our regular cook had to be airlifted to a hospital with appendicitis."

Stevi laughed softly, and despite all her previous lectures to herself she asked, "You mean you worked on an oil rig before you did this?"

"For almost thirteen years, and before that I worked the family ranch."

"In Texas."

The lines at the corners of his eyes deepened with his amusement. "I guess my drawl gave me away."

The look in his eyes was so tender, the part of Stevi that was starving for affection and compassion trembled with pleasure. But realizing how dangerous that was, she quickly dropped her gaze to her plate, and with an inaudible sigh jabbed her fork into a piece of gravy-soaked biscuit.

"Did you sleep all right?"

"Yes." Surprisingly. Despite being in an unfamiliar place, she'd slept through the night, and without having one of her nightmares. "Thank you for the use of the apartment. Is the artwork yours?"

Over the rim of his mug he watched sunlight refract in her eyes, the way it did in the deepest waters, and wondered how many men had lost themselves in their indigo depths. "I wish I could claim they were; they're good, aren't they? But no, O'Neal was the one who could take a piece of rotting driftwood and see more. Sweet and I met him when we were doing a job in the Middle East, and I don't think I can remember a time when he didn't have a knife and a piece of wood in his hands." Dane saw the curiosity in Stevi's eyes, but sensed she wouldn't ask the questions. "You're wondering how we all got from there to here. Well, O'Neal took early retirement—his wife had diabetes, and when her condition grew serious he wanted to be able to be with her. He used his savings to buy the café and add on the lounge. But a few years later Doris passed away and he started to lose interest in the place. He'd kept in touch through the years and one day I received a letter asking if Sweet and I wanted to buy in. The oil industry had become more of a roller-coaster ride than a business, and political unrest was perpetually following wherever we were working, so we decided it might be a healthier way to make a living. O'Neal and Doris never had any kids, and when he died, he left everything to Sweet and me. We used our original capital investment and built on the motel."

"You speak casually about the friendship you've shared and yet it was, is, so obviously special."

"My mother always told me it wasn't nice to brag." Dane caught her mouth twitching, though she ducked her head to concentrate on wiping her hands in her napkin. "I've been wondering—is Stevi your real name?"

After placing the napkin back in her lap, her fingers stilled. "Real enough. It's what people always preferred to call me instead of Stephanie."

"You sound like a native. Are you?"

"More or less."

"That's a mysterious answer."

"Not at all." With a calmness that was sheer bravado, she lifted her head to meet his searching gaze. "It simply means that I've called many parts of the state home."

"Army brat?"

"Pardon?"

"Was it because your family got transferred around a lot?"

"No. I—I just like to travel, that's all."

Dane didn't buy that. "You want to talk about it?"

"No."

He could have been annoyed with the way she abruptly shut him out, but beneath that cool facade he sensed nerves that should have been humming, they seemed so taut. He wanted to reach over and lay a reassuring hand over hers. He wanted to tell her she had nothing to fear from him. But even as the impulse was checked, he knew it wouldn't be entirely the truth.

Maybe she *should* worry about him a little. Granted, whatever problem it was she had, he didn't want to make it worse, but he also knew he was attracted. It wasn't something he was finding easy to ignore. She'd been the last thing on his mind when he went to bed last night, and when he'd opened his eyes this morning, the first thing he thought of. He knew it was partly because she was being so damned mysterious about herself that she defied a person's imagination *not* to spin theories about her. But she was also beautiful, and sexy, and she stirred feelings in him that had been dormant for a long time.

"Stevi, I—"

"Did you—"

"Excuse me," Dane said, inclining his head. "You first."

She hadn't really wanted to say anything, but the silence between them was growing increasingly uncomfortable and it encouraged her to break her own rules in order to redirect his attention. "I was only going to ask if you ever go back to your family's ranch?"

"No, I haven't been back in a while." He sometimes thought about it. The letters Delia sent him were coming more frequently and it was obvious that the economy was having its effect on her marriage to Clay as well as on the ranch. It was hardly nuance that she was having second thoughts about having married the wrong brother, after all. "There's only my older brother and my sister-in-law left, and Clay and I were always too competitive to spend much time around each other without causing friction. What about you? Do you ever get tired of all your traveling and go home to visit your family?''

She shook her head and sat back, replete although there was still plenty of food left on her plate. "They're all gone now," she explained cautiously, as she gauged what was safe to tell him. "My parents died when I was a baby and I was raised by my aunt and uncle. My uncle died when I was barely twenty and my aunt passed away a few years later."

The dog interrupted whatever other conversation would have followed by choosing that moment to rise from the cool linoleum floor and, wandering over to Stevi, lay its large head in her lap. This time the topaz eyes that gazed into hers were anything but threatening.

"I call him Bear," Dane murmured. "Guess he recognizes one of his own. He's a stray, too."

Stevi tried to repress her rising amusement, but Bear raised a paw as if suddenly remembering his manners, and she gave into a short, throaty laugh. "Is it all right if I feed him?"

"Let's put it this way: he won't let you out of there until you do."

"In that case, here," she told the dog, handing it a piece of gravy-soaked biscuit. Bit by bit Bear ate the scraps she offered him, careful with his teeth. But when he realized there was no more, he quickly abandoned her to move to Dane's side.

"Don't look at me, you overgrown vulture. I ate mine. Go let yourself out and run off some of that food."

Stevi watched in amazement as the dog did exactly as directed, using his paw to force the handle of the screen door, then pushing the door open with his nose. "That's incredible," she murmured, bubbling with laughter. "Can he get back in?"

"Mmm—though not as successfully. I've had to repair that screen twice this summer alone." Watching her, Dane felt a pull deep in his belly that, if he hadn't already eaten, he might have mistaken for hunger. On second thought, he decided, it was hunger—of a kind: the hunger to have her look at him and know *he* put those stars in her eyes; the hunger to run his lips down the graceful column of her throat, down and beyond the three buttons of her top. He took a deep breath to rein in his unruly thoughts. "Would you like another cup of coffee?"

Feeling the pull, the crazy, unreasonable attraction she'd sensed last night, Stevi shook her head and reached for her wallet. "I'd better be going."

"Going where?"

"Well, I need to find a place to stay, for one thing."

"You have a place to stay."

As she uncurled her legs, Stevi found herself blocked in by his. "You only meant for me to use the place for the night because it was late."

"Did I?"

The low rumble of his voice caused her heartbeat to accelerate until it pounded frenetically against her breast. "Please let me go."

"You're welcome to stay next door."

"It's more than I need," she replied, looking everywhere but at him. "Besides, I couldn't possibly afford to pay the rent on it."

"What can you afford?"

When she reluctantly mentioned a figure in proportion to the salary they'd agreed upon last night, he inclined his head in acceptance.

"Fine. We have a deal. Shall we shake on it instead of writing up a contract?"

Stevi glanced from his extended hand to his face. "You know you could get twice that."

"I'm not interested in the money, I'm interested in helping you out."

She redirected her gaze to the connecting doors between their apartments she'd discovered last night. "And perhaps yourself in the process?"

Muttering an oath beneath his breath, Dane rose and headed for the door. "Come here." When she failed to move, he banked his impatience and repeated his request in a more polite tone of voice. "I want you to see something."

Reluctantly Stevi followed. But she stopped several steps away from him, not so much because she thought she needed to be careful around him, but because she wasn't certain about her own feelings. They were virtual strangers, and yet she wanted to believe in him so badly.

"Yesterday when I told you to wait until you're asked, I suppose I should also have pointed out that I don't trespass where I'm not invited. This door has to be unlocked from both sides before it'll budge. See?"

Stevi closed her eyes in sheer embarrassment.

"Use the apartment," Dane urged quietly.

"Yes, all right." Knowing she had to get out of there before she made an even bigger fool of herself by starting to cry, she took a backward step. "Thank you, for breakfast and for—everything." At the screen door she hesitated and glanced back to find he hadn't moved.

The intensity of his look made her mouth turn dry. "I know you must think I'm crazy," she began, feeling she owed him something. "But I do have my reasons."

He already knew that; he needed to know what they were. "Stevi—do I have to worry about the police coming to look for you?"

Outside, a speckled woodpecker flew to a pine tree and began hunting for food, but she didn't see it. She didn't see anything except the bleakness of her own future. "No," she murmured. "Not the police."

Chapter Three

This section of tables and those booths will be yours," Marge said, running through the routine with Stevi later that evening. "Oh, and of course that means you get Henri, too."

Stevi paused midway in smoothing down her hand-painted, beaded top. "What do you mean, I 'get' Henri?"

"You bring him his drinks."

"Oh."

"He likes rum and Cokes. Sweet seems to be able to tell when he's ready. You'll want to remember to leave the swizzle sticks when you replace his glass with a new one. Henri swears he tells time that way." Marge rolled her eyes.

Stevi nodded; she'd heard of stranger eccentricities. Glancing down at her outfit, the top and black jeans she'd changed into and out of a half-dozen times, she wondered again if it wasn't too much. She compared it to Marge's T-shirt with the comic-strip character emblazoned on the front. "Are you sure I shouldn't go change?"

"Don't be silly. We don't have a dress code here. Good thing, too, because I didn't have time to do the wash today and I had to borrow this from my sixteen-year-old son. I *love* your top, especially that parrot. Wherever did you buy it?"

"It was a gift from a friend."

Seeing something sad flicker briefly in Stevi's eyes, Marge frowned and quickly took her arm. "Here comes Penny and it looks like she's been baking again. I hope it's brownies; her brownies will send you straight to heaven."

Stevi held back. "Why don't you go on and I'll check with that couple over there to see if they're ready for another round."

"You give them another round and they'll be under the table before anyone else gets here."

"But—"

"Don't you want something to eat?"

She would love to have something to eat. The cheeseburger she'd bought herself for dinner was delicious and had been devoured all too quickly. Still, she didn't want to intrude—for more reasons than she wanted to explain. "Maybe there won't be enough," she murmured, hedging.

Marge linked her arm completely around Stevi's and determinedly marched her toward the bar where Sweet was already relieving Penny of the plastic container she was carrying. "Two things you'd better learn right off, kiddo: one is that you're family now and whether you like it or not, you're stuck with us; and two is that Penny is the reason why Sweet and I could double as

Mr. and Mrs. Santa Claus at Christmastime. Now stop being so darned polite and come on over here."

That was how Stevi found herself adopted by the group. And even though she doubted it was a good idea and remained almost as quiet as Penny, she enjoyed listening to their good-natured teasing and basked in the warmth they exuded as they displayed their affection for each other. One by one the others arrived: Jolene, who insisted she didn't mind working a double shift though she wasn't due to start until next week; Henri, resplendent tonight in a red bow tie, suspenders, and a red-and-white striped shirt; and Dane, who surprised Stevi by doing nothing more than giving her a friendly greeting before teasing Marge outrageously about her T-shirt. They made short work of Penny's brownies and shared anecdotes of whatever experiences they'd had since seeing each other last night.

Finally, as more customers arrived, the group dispersed. Once again Dane surprised Stevi by simply wishing her luck and referring her to Sweet or Marge if she had any questions or problems. Then he retreated to his office, leaving her to stand there wondering if she should be relieved or disappointed.

"Another pitcher of beer and three Seven and Sevens," Marge told Sweet as she laid her tray on the bar. Taking advantage of the break, she sat down on the empty stool beside her and groaned while rubbing her sore feet. "When am I going to learn that I wear a size-eight shoe and not a seven and a half? You'd think at my age I'd have outgrown my vanities."

"It'll get worse before it gets better," Sweet said philosophically.

"Who asked you, you overgrown hippie." She turned to Stevi, who came up to the bar and gave Sweet her own order. "How's it going?"

"I keep trying to serve bourbon to a man who drinks Scotch, and the lady with the fluorescent blue eye shadow is accusing me of serving her watered-down drinks. Other than that, I think I'm getting the hang of it."

"Considering Thursdays are turning out to be almost as busy as Fridays, I think you're doing fine. My first night—"

"Now, Marge," Sweet interrupted, grinning as he placed the pitcher of beer on her tray, "you know you can't remember that far back."

She reached across the counter and tried to grab a handful of his beard, only to send a bowl of peanuts skittering farther down the bar. "Come here, you. I dare you to say that again."

Stevi caught the bowl and managed to keep a straight face. It hadn't taken her long to figure out they played like this all the time. "Time-out. At least wait until I get my order filled before you strangle him."

Sweet feigned an indignant sound. "Thanks a lot!"

Chuckling, Stevi shook her head and turned to watch Henri at the piano. An unusual man, she decided, wondering what was really going on behind those wire-framed glasses. Because of the blues he'd been playing for the last half hour, she guessed the others would judge him to be in a good mood. However, when he suddenly slipped into an old Willie Nelson favorite, she shot Marge a look of confusion.

Laughing, the older woman slipped off the stool and picked up her tray. "Got you that time, did he? That's only his signal to Dane to let him know it's ten o'clock.

The boss likes to come out a couple of times a night to mingle and check things out. See?''

The office door opened and Dane stepped out. Stevi observed most of the women in the room take notice. She couldn't blame them; wearing stone-washed jeans and a white dress shirt with the sleeves rolled up, he looked both powerful and handsome—an irresistible combination for any woman.

She watched as he moved around the room, pausing, shaking hands, his smile relaxed, friendly. He was, she decided, a man who cared about people. She could have done a lot worse by not getting off the bus when she did.

"You're up, kiddo."

"What?" Stevi spun around to find Sweet pushing her drink-laden tray toward her. "Oh—right. Whew." She whistled softly, taking a second whiff of one of the drinks she didn't remember ordering. "Whose is this?"

"Henri's."

"I hope he has a cast-iron belly."

"He does, and a hollow leg."

She delivered his drink last. He was just ending a song when she arrived.

"I was hoping that was for me," he said, lifting the glass from her tray himself. He took a long sip and made a sound of ecstasy. "You've saved my life. Tell me what you'd like to hear next. Any song, it's yours."

"Is there a Henri Chennault original in your repertoire?"

Smiling, he pushed his slipping glasses back up his nose. "I knew there was something about you I liked the moment I saw you. 'Henri,' I said to myself, 'now there's a young woman with excellent taste.'"

"*And* who's immune to flattery."

"That's okay. I just used my one good line. Besides, I'd much rather talk about me."

"You're strange," Stevi said, chuckling. "But definitely talented."

"Two songs. Keep it up and we'll be here all night."

"Can I get that in writing?" Dane asked dryly as he stepped up to the piano beside Stevi. He gave her a wink and explained, "These days he's usually off the piano by midnight and on the phone with his agent."

"You know he's on the road a lot," Henri said, unperturbed. "It's the only time I can get hold of him."

Dane nodded, having heard it all before, and eyed the younger man speculatively. "You know one of these days I won't take you back."

Henri grinned. "One of these days I won't *be* back."

"Er—is there something you needed me for, Mr. Randolph?" Stevi asked, unsure how serious this bantering was and wanting to end it before it got out of hand.

"Mr. Randolph?" Henri ran his tongue along the inside of his cheek. "You'd better cut that out before he decides he likes the sound of it and demands the rest of us to conform accordingly."

"Behave," Dane muttered, before turning to Stevi. "Actually, I only wanted to tell Henri that the Nylands were requesting something romantic to dance to." His eyes told her he wouldn't mind dancing himself, with her.

"In that case—" her throat suddenly went dry and she swallowed heavily "—I'd better get back to work."

"Don't rush off on his account," Henri drawled.

"It's time to check on my other tables."

Dane captured her gaze once more. "You're looking a little tired. Be sure to take your breaks."

"Yes. All right."

Henri watched her hurry away. "My compliments," he said, just loudly enough for his employer to hear. "She certainly improves the scenery around here."

Dane's dark eyes lost all traces of amusement. "Don't even think it. Stevi's not the type for brief flings."

"I'm flattered that you have any such concerns, but you know I put all my passion into my music."

Dane knew, and he felt like a fool for saying anything. But it had bothered him to see Stevi chatting so easily with Henri when it was obvious she would do anything to avoid *him*.

"Where's she from?" Henri asked, after taking another sip of his drink.

"I don't know. She got off the bus that came through last night."

"Where was she headed? Surely not here?"

"I don't know that, either."

Henri raised a tawny eyebrow. "Well, what *do* you know about her?"

"Next to nothing," Dane admitted, turning to watch her help Penny carry a large drink order. But things weren't going to stay that way for long, he promised himself. "Don't forget the Nylands' song," he reminded Henri, and headed for the bar.

The weekend passed in a blur for Stevi, and before she knew it she'd completed her first week at O'Neal's. She also began to feel a sense of confidence about her work. It might not be the way she'd imagined herself earning a living, but at least it was honest and physically demanding work. Each night she dropped into bed, falling asleep immediately. And though she continued to have the nightmares, they weren't on a nightly basis, and most of the time she could even go back to sleep after a while.

Sweet, Marge and the others continued to make her feel welcome. It began to get easier to avoid their questions about her past, especially when she learned to use the tactic of encouraging them to talk about themselves. But that, in a way, created its own problem: the better she got to know them, the more she grew to care about them. Nowhere did that apply more than with Dane.

He was proving to be an absolute gentleman. A day didn't go by when he didn't do something to reaffirm that, whether it was to work on Penny's car at two in the morning, or to pick up the tab for an elderly couple when he discovered it was their fortieth wedding anniversary. One day she even witnessed him intervene on Jesse's behalf when a carload of teenage boys pulled into the gas station and began heckling the old man.

Equally effectual in gaining her trust in him was discovering that he was a man of his word. He soon made it clear he'd meant what he told her that first morning in his kitchen: he didn't trespass where he wasn't invited. The door between their apartments remained locked. His attitude toward her remained congenial but hardly intimate. She should have been relieved, even content, but her feelings were hardly that clear-cut.

Knowing she would drive herself crazy dwelling on thoughts like that, she did her best to keep herself busy. At first that wasn't easy. Her half of the duplex required little cleaning, and she hand-washed her clothes on a daily basis, which only took a few minutes. Taking long walks and exploring the woods along the lake was enjoyable, though safer when Bear came along to spot snakes, and it was best left to the mornings when it was cooler. That still netted her several hours of free time a day.

When she first mentioned that to Dane and asked if there was something she could do, he asked her if she'd been in the sun too long.

"Stevi, you already put in an eight-hour day. I won't ask you to do more. Kick back. Help yourself to my books. Relax."

"*You* don't. You're always saying the day isn't long enough to do everything you need to do. Let me help."

"Can you replace the gutters, which I have to do, or rework the lawn mower Sweet has to get to before the back turns into a jungle?"

"No," she admitted. Then she brightened. "But I can finish cleaning up the lounge and restock things the way Sweet does every afternoon. That would free him to do the more difficult projects."

Dane still resisted and in the end Stevi went directly to Sweet to plead her case. Never a great fan of tedious chores, the gentle giant found her idea a good one and gratefully agreed.

When Dane walked into the lounge the following day and found her carrying a tray of glasses from the dishwasher to the bar, there was a moment when she thought she might drop everything. His expression went from surprised to stormy.

"Damn it, Stevi, I was serious when I said no, yesterday."

"Please don't be angry," she said, quickly setting the tray on the bar. "I can explain."

"What's to explain? It's obvious you plan to do whatever you like, no matter what I say."

Stevi came around the bar, gripping a dish towel. "You don't understand; I wasn't raised to play the lady of leisure."

"You're right, I don't. How can I when you've made it clear no one's allowed to ask you anything about who you are or where you come from." An instant later he turned away, uttering something unintelligible under his breath. Wearily he rubbed the back of his neck. "That was uncalled-for, I'm sorry. It's just that you get to me, you know? You walk in here looking lost and afraid of your own shadow, looking like you've been living on half rations and about as substantial as an umbrella in a hurricane. And then when you're already pulling your weight around here, you decide to take on a double load. Hell, I want to help you, not turn you into slave labor."

"Maybe what you don't understand is that by letting me pay you back for taking me on you *are* helping me," she told him, keeping her eyes downcast. "I know I look like a lightweight, but I'm tougher than you think."

He didn't know whether to laugh or swear. "I'm beginning to realize that." Something in his voice brought her gaze up to meet his. "I should fire you. I have a feeling this isn't the last time you'll make up your own rules."

"But you won't." The hint of a smile warmed her eyes.

No, he wouldn't. He was already caught up in her, and whether she liked it or not, intrigued. "Don't push your luck. The first time I see you sleeping on your feet during your shift, you're out. I won't stand by and watch you kill yourself, either."

She burst into laughter. She didn't mean to; it was probably just relief or a rush of pleasure at having someone care enough to *want* to treat her as though she were special. Whatever the reason, it burst from her like sunlight breaking free from a storm cloud.

Dane felt the warmth of it seep through every pore of his body. He took a step closer. "Stevi—"

As the front door opened, a shaft of daylight momentarily blinded them both.

"Hey, you two!" Henri Chennault sped by them on his way to the piano. "Listen up. You're about to have the scintillating pleasure of hearing my newest masterpiece."

Dane barely spared the excited man a glance; he was too intent on watching Stevi, watching the walls of caution and reserve return. But he could also see that she understood what would have happened if Henri hadn't chosen this moment to intrude.

"Later," he promised, heading for the door.

"Okay, sure," Henri mumbled, setting his music in place and making an adjustment with the pencil he took from behind his ear.

Only Stevi understood that it hadn't been Henri Dane had been speaking to.

She listened to Henri's composition and gave him the compliments he expected and deserved. Afterward, she returned to her own work while he fine-tuned the piece. When she was finished with the glasses, she eyed the storage shelves at the back. They looked as if someone had left the back door open during the last storm: there was no semblance of order, and boxes that had been ripped open during a search for an item were left hanging half off the shelves waiting for the slightest movement to send them spilling their contents to the floor.

"Men," Stevi muttered to herself. Her uncle had been no different and her aunt had often declared that there wasn't a man born who could be counted on to put things back where they belonged. Well, she thought, rubbing her hands along her jeans-clad thighs, let Dane fuss if he wanted; here was a job that needed doing.

She wasn't sure how long it took her; lost in her work, she was barely aware of Henri sliding from one piece into another, or that as he began to run through some of the songs he sang during his sets, she began to hum along. When she was finished, she tossed the empty boxes into the trash container and scooped up the box of swizzle sticks she knew Sweet could use up front.

Henri was back to his new composition again, and by the way he was pounding the keys she could tell something was wrong. "What's the matter?" she asked, transferring the stirrers to the nearly empty container under the bar. "I thought you were pleased with the piece?"

"I thought I was." Scowling, he ran through a few bars again. "Am I crazy or does that sound forced there?"

"Maybe a little," she replied honestly. "You could always try it without the flourish. It's a love song, right? Keep it simple. Let the words carry their share of the workload."

Henri stared at her for a moment and then down at the score sheet. He read through the bars again, nodding his head in time, and suddenly grunted in surprise. Whipping the pencil from between his compressed lips, he frantically erased and scrawled in his changes. Then he replayed the piece. "Hey, yeah! Thanks."

Stevi smiled dreamily, listening. "It's a lovely piece. Especially the chorus. 'In your eyes, my dreams are always there. In your eyes...'" Forgetting the rest of the words, she began to hum them until Henri joined in to help her. Mesmerized by the lyrical beauty of the piece she edged closer. Henri shifted over, indicating that she should sit down, and she joined him on the bench, and in finishing the song.

He watched her fingers reach for the piano keys, the movement impulsive, but quickly checked. "Do it for me," he said getting up and crossing over to the bar.

She blinked, as if coming out of a trance. "Oh, I couldn't."

"I want to know what it really sounds like. Please, do it for me. I know you can."

Stevi looked down at the piano, felt the pull she'd been resisting for days now, and knew what an addict must feel like when tempted by the forbidden. But what would it hurt if she played it just once? There was only Henri here, and he would keep her secret if she asked him to. She placed her fingertips on the keys and began to play.

It came easily. It always had—ever since her aunt had sat her down at that old upright in the church when she was five. And it felt wonderful, cleansing, like the hymns they would sing on Sundays. Denying herself her music had cost her; the strength and peace she derived from playing had always been a sustaining one. It was again.

When the last notes died away, she sat there wishing she could play it again, and then continue until she'd played every song she'd ever learned. But she knew she was risking enough already. Smiling sadly, she looked up, about to tell Henri that he had to make a recording of this. She was sure it would give him the break he was looking for. But the smile on her face was immediately replaced by a look of dismay.

"My God," Henri said at last, still sitting in stunned disbelief. "You're terrific! Why on earth aren't you doing something with that talent?"

Stevi couldn't have answered if she'd wanted to; her throat locked the moment she realized they weren't alone. Dane stood in the doorway of his office; and from the expression on his face, she could tell he'd heard more than enough.

Chapter Four

That's exactly what I was going to ask," Dane murmured, breaking the long stretch of silence that followed. He decided the most readable expression on
Stevi's face was guilt. Served her right, the little fraud.
But why the fear?

"I—I thought you'd left," she said, her voice reed
thin, barely recognizable from the one that had captured his attention a few moments ago.

"I came back." He'd received a call from one of his
suppliers about an invoice discrepancy and he'd gone to
his office to check the books. He thought she'd been the
one to leave. Even when he first heard her sing, he
hadn't made the connection; he'd assumed Henri had
turned on the stereo and was playing a tape. But he'd
been instantly captivated by that voice. It was a little
husky, sexy. A voice like that would really bring in the
business, he'd mused wistfully, tempted to go out and
ask Henri who the singer was. Seconds later, when he

realized it was the same song he'd heard Henri practicing, it struck him that he *did* know the voice. It was Stevi's. "You're very good," he added. "But then I don't suppose you need me to tell you that."

She shrugged, averting her eyes so he couldn't see the hurt she felt at the accusation underlying his words. "It's always nice to hear when someone thinks you have talent."

Henri snapped out of his trance and came toward her. "Talent, nothing. You could be a star!"

"It takes more than ability to be a star," she replied, rising. "You of all people should understand that. It takes persistence, luck, and an all-out hunger for it. I'm afraid I'm not that ambitious."

"Who taught you to play?" Dane asked.

"My aunt." At least that much she could tell him about herself. "She was the pianist for our church and she used to take me with her when she went to practice for Sunday services. By the time I was ten, I could play any hymn in the songbooks."

"Have you ever played anywhere other than church?"

Stevi turned back to Henri, maintaining a calm that was only skin-deep. "Occasionally."

"Want to double up with me some night?"

She would as soon put a full-page ad in the paper announcing her whereabouts. "Thanks, but as I've explained, I'm not interested in pursuing a career." Excusing herself, she made a beeline for the door. Maybe, she told herself, just maybe they would leave it at that.

But her nerves were a mess, and needing to calm them she walked down to the dock. Out in the water a family of turtles were climbing onto a log to soak up the early-afternoon sun. A dragonfly settled on a lily pad. Stevi leaned against the wooden railing at the end of the dock and closed her eyes, willing herself to absorb some of the surrounding tranquillity. A subtle throbbing was already starting at her temple. Sighing, she gently massaged the spot.

"The trouble with having too many secrets is that they have a tendency to do that to you."

Stevi didn't jump. Somehow she'd known he would follow her. Glancing over her shoulder, she found him leaning against the security-light pole, his arms crossed, his expression impassive. She lowered her fingers to her throat and felt the flurry of her pulse.

"Was stalking people something you learned on those oil rigs?"

"Are you feeling stalked?"

"No, cornered."

Pushing away from the pole, he came toward her, then rested a hand on either side of the railing to box her in. "Now you are."

"Dane—" Stevi closed her eyes. He was too close. "Please don't."

"Don't what?" His breath feathered her bangs. "Don't ask you any more questions? Or don't kiss you the way you know I would have if Henri hadn't decided to make an appearance?"

"Both," she whispered, turning her head away.

For a moment he let his gaze wander over her face and let desire battle it out with conscience. He wanted to know if her skin felt as soft as it looked, if the taste of sugar still clung to her lips from that doughnut he'd seen her eat this morning. But conscience won out and he forced himself to back away. Stepping over to the other side of the dock, he rested his forearms on the wooden rail and looked down into the water to watch a small school of bream in a patch of shade.

Stevi moistened her lips. "Do you want me to leave?"

He shot her an eloquent look.

"I know you're angry."

"Stevi, I'm not— I don't know what I am." He sighed, his frustration palpable. "How's that for an answer? It's almost as incoherent as some of yours." He caught her faint wince and swore softly. "You're right. That was an unfair dig."

"You're disappointed in me, I understand."

"I don't think you do." Nor, at this point, could he tell her she was turning his world upside down in a way even Delia hadn't managed. He knew she wasn't ready to hear something like that. He wasn't sure he was ready himself. "I thought we were building a basis of trust?"

"This has nothing to do with trust." Accepting that she would be forced to stay on the defensive, she managed a brief laugh. "All right, I can play the piano and carry a tune. So what? I hardly thought it pertinent to tell you, since you already have Henri and I wasn't applying for his job in the first place."

Dane lifted a brow. "Honey, you do more than carry a tune." Her demure murmur of thanks caused an increasingly familiar tug beneath his ribs. "Why were you terrified when you looked up and saw me?"

"I was surprised, not frightened."

She was shutting him out and that hurt. It made him feel foolish for thinking there might be something special growing between them. "Is it always going to be one step forward and two back with you?"

"I don't understand," she replied, hedging.

"The more I learn about you, the more the questions keep piling up."

Stevi's answering look was direct but mournful. "Leave it alone, cowboy. Just think of me as no one coming from noplace and headed nowhere. Accept that and we'll both stay a lot happier."

Dane shoved his hands into his pockets to resist a strong urge to reach out, grab her, and show her how wrong she was. "You've got a strange idea of happiness, Stevi."

This time he was the one to walk away, but he found it no easier.

Stevi closed her eyes against the threat of tears. It's better this way, she told herself. He couldn't know it, but she was actually doing him a favor. He might end up despising her, but at least he would be alive. It was a lesson she had learned the hard way; if she had accepted control and made her own decisions sooner, Paul might still be alive, too.

As she headed for the duplex, she hoped that at least the worst between them was over, and yet she wasn't naive enough to count on it.

If the first week at O'Neal's flew by, the second crawled at a snail's pace. The following Thursday afternoon found Stevi behind the bar, listening as Sweet ran her through yet another drink recipe. She'd talked him into giving her the lessons by convincing him it would be an asset to have two bartenders available if things got very busy. The real reason, though, was that it helped her to get her mind off her troubles.

"Okay, let's see if I've got this straight," she said, rubbing her palms together. "If I'm making a mint julep, I use bourbon. When I use gin, it becomes a Major Bailey. I *can* make it with champagne, but then I have to increase the ratio of bubbly and add a dash of brandy." She paused, then tapped her finger against the bottle of rum on the rack. "What am I forgetting about this?"

"Some people like to touch off their juleps with a dash of rum."

"No wonder you see most people sitting down when they're drinking these. Ever get the urge to warn people about what they're doing to their livers?"

"Sure, and I've done it. Abuse and excess in anything are unhealthy, and it's a good bartender who pays attention to his customers so he can suggest they shut it off when he thinks they've had enough."

"I suppose so."

"But the real trick to being a good bartender is listening, Stevi, and you certainly have that talent."

Feeling guilty because she knew it was mostly a ploy she used to keep from talking about herself, she shook her head. "Not really."

"Yes, you do. I've seen you with Marge and the others. You let them rattle on about their kids and grandkids—Penny could drive a body crazy, what with the way she goes on and on about how she likes to snap her string beans this way for a salad and that way for a casserole; but you keep listening and looking at her like it all made good sense."

"She's lonely," Stevi reminded him. "All she has is her hypochondriac mother who won't leave the house except to go to church on Sunday."

"Aw, I'm not picking on her. Shoot, I have plenty of my own strange ways." Sweet glanced up from the supply list he was working on to watch her flip through a few more of his recipe cards. "Er, by the way, I've been meaning to ask you something. Do you think I should cut my hair?"

Having acquired a wariness for people who said "Can I ask you something?" Stevi was doubly surprised to hear Sweet's question. "Why? It suits you. Next you'll be telling me you've been thinking about shaving off your beard."

His expression grew mournful as he stroked it. "Well, I'd hate to, but then I think about how good Dane looked after he shaved off his."

Dane in a full beard... Stevi tried to picture it and decided that with his dark, intense eyes, unless he smiled a lot, he would have looked like an outlaw: intimidating. "It's usually a bad idea to do something like that just because you think someone else looks good. What's the real reason, Sweet?"

"You're not gonna laugh now, are you?"

Though the lounge was dimly lit, she could see his cheeks were already turning pink. "Not unless you tell me you want to get a perm and wear your hair like Marge's."

"Wouldn't need any perm." He chuckled, running a hand over his frizzy ponytail. Then he sighed. "It's Jolene's youngest. I scared him the other day.

"You know she brought in that toaster I said I'd try to fix. Well, I finished it yesterday and thought she might need it before she came in to work, so I drove over to her place to bring it to her. He was playing out front when I pulled up in my pickup. Took one look and ran off bawling like I was the bogeyman come to get him."

"Oh, Sweet—" Stevi leaned over and laid her hand over his in sympathy "—I don't think it was *you*. You know Jolene's husband died not long ago. She told me that even though they'd been separated he'd kept coming to the trailer to harass her and the boys. From what she's said about him, I don't think he was a pleasant man, and if I understood her correctly, he drove a pickup similar to yours."

"He did? I didn't know that." He drew his teeth over his lower lip. "Maybe I ought to just repaint my truck."

"For Joey or Jolene?" she teased, putting two and two together.

Such was the scene that greeted Dane as he came through the front door: Stevi and Sweet clasping hands, laughing in a way *he* and Stevi never did. It brought him to the conclusion that this was turning out to be a thoroughly lousy day.

Scowling, he strode over to the bar and sat down. "Do one of you think you could pour me a bourbon, or would three be a crowd?"

As soon as he saw the way Stevi seemed to recoil, he regretted his sarcasm. They hadn't talked much since that day on the dock, and whatever annoyance and frustration he'd felt toward her was long gone. But he'd continued to keep his distance because he thought that was the way she wanted it. Up until this moment, he hadn't wanted to admit that that was a big part of the reason why he was feeling edgy and resentful.

"What's got you wired?" Sweet muttered, pouring a double and setting it before him in a way that almost spilled half of it on the countertop.

Hoping that the alcohol would do something to ease his short temper, Dane took a healthy swallow first. Because he hadn't had much of an appetite these past few days, his stomach was virtually empty and he felt the burning immediately and was grateful for it.

"Henri's gone," he rasped, after downing the rest of the bourbon.

Sweet caught himself before muttering a curse, cast Stevi a guilty look and opted to snap his pencil in two. "That little weasel. Where's he off to this time?"

"New Orleans. He won't be back, Sweet. Not only did he sign a long-term contract with a club in the French Quarter, his agent thinks he may have him a recording contract."

"But that's wonderful!" Stevi cried. "You should be happy for him. It's what he's always dreamed of."

Dane gestured for Sweet to refill his glass before he ran his fingers over his mustache. "Well, honey, it's a bit hard to cheer with your throat cut. Henri's good fortune means that I'm without an entertainer, and the weekend's coming up, which means there's a fishing tournament coming to the lake. The motel is booked solid, and when those boys come in here to party, stereo music just doesn't cut it."

"What did you do when he left all those other times you mentioned?" Stevi asked.

"Lost money," Sweet replied.

The three of them fell silent. Stevi decided she still couldn't blame Henri for grabbing an opportunity when it presented itself, but she also understood the problems that made for those he left behind. No wonder Dane had been grouchy when he came in. She peered at him from under her lashes only to discover that he was looking at her in a way she didn't think she liked.

"What?" she demanded.

"You."

"Me, what?"

"You can take his place."

She felt her knees give beneath her and grabbed behind her to clutch at the back counter to steady herself.

"You can't be serious." But she could see he was. "I can't," she said, shaking her head emphatically.

Frowning, Sweet looked from Stevi's blanched face to Dane's determined one. "What's the matter with you? We don't even know if she can play the piano."

"Yes, we do, and she can," Dane replied, keeping Stevi pinned in place with his steady gaze.

"But I *won't*." Though her hands continued to tremble, her voice grew firm.

"Stevi, I need you."

That was the last thing she wanted to hear. "You don't know what you're asking."

"I'm asking you to save my neck. All our necks, for that matter."

And in the process maybe put her own in a noose, but there was no way she could explain that to him. "Look, it can't be that hard to find a replacement. Place an ad in the paper. Run a contest."

"I need a professional, not some amateur whose parents told them they had talent."

"Then call an employment agency."

"We've tried that before," Sweet told her. "People like the place well enough, but not our location. It makes them kind of antsy, you know?"

Stevi loved the location and the quietness, but she knew if she took the job, it was a good bet things weren't going to stay that way. At the same time, she knew she owed Dane. He'd given her a job, a place to live at a ridiculously low rent. He'd offered her his friendship. She wasn't paying him back very well.

Torn between the converse pulls of her heart and her head, she rubbed her brow. "I don't want to be put in this position."

"I wouldn't ask if it wasn't important."

"I know." She wet her dry lips. "It's just— I prefer a quieter life-style these days."

"I'm not asking you for a long-term commitment." God, Dane thought, she was going to drive him crazy wondering what this was all about. "You'd only be filling in until I could find someone else."

"Really?"

"If that's what you want."

"And no ad in the parish paper like the one you do for Henri?"

Dane dropped his head into his hands a moment before raking them through his hair. "Contrary to what you might think, I *am* in this business to make a profit." If he'd blinked, he would have missed the betraying tremor of her lips. His heart, wanting a truce at any cost, surrendered. "Okay—" he sighed "—no ad."

Now I've done it, Stevi thought, raising her clenched hands to her lips. She couldn't keep tossing stipulations at him in the hope that he would give up. He wouldn't. She didn't blame him, either. And she wanted to help him, she really did. It was only...

"All right," she said on impulse. "I'll do it—but *only* until you find someone else."

He could have kissed her; he settled for wishing she didn't look at him in a way that made him feel as though the white hat she'd delegated him to wear had just been kicked in the dirt.

"Thanks, Stevi." He knew there was no way Sweet wasn't going to pick up on the tenderness in his voice, but at this point he didn't care. "You won't regret this."

Stevi's answering look spoke fathoms. "Don't make promises you may not be able to keep."

Dane had asked her if she could start that night, and a few hours later, after showering and drying her hair, Stevi slipped into one of the few dresses she'd packed in her suitcase. It was a pencil-slim sheath the color of claret with delicately braided shoulder straps. A favorite, she hadn't worn it in over two months and couldn't help but enjoy feeling silk against her body again; yet along with that came the inevitable memories, and as she stood before the bathroom mirror and put the finishing touches on her makeup, she wondered again at the wisdom of what she was doing.

She could have said no. She could have left— O'Neal's, Bayou Landing, all of it. The farther she went, the better her chances would be to stay lost. But then Dane had looked at her in that certain way and told her he needed her.

She muttered a word in the Cajun dialect her uncle had been partial to whenever he was feeling particularly disgusted with himself. "Stevi," she warned the young woman who looked back at her from the vanity mirror. "You can't stay within reaching distance of the devil and not tempt him."

But she couldn't walk out on Dane, either.

A knock at her door brought her out of her brooding. She quickly replaced the blusher brush back into its compact and gave her reflection one more critical glance. "Show time," she murmured drolly and flicked off the light switch.

It was Jolene at the door. "Dane thought I should come over and give you some moral— Wow!"

Stevi smiled, understanding. Her aunt used to wear that same awed yet slightly dubious look, too. But back then it was because she'd known Stevi despised the man she had to work for. "Thanks for coming. Dane's right; I could use some support."

Stepping inside, Jolene made a full circle around her. "And here I thought you were on the shy side, like me." She caught Stevi's look and waved a hand in dismissal. "Oh, I know my mouth runs all the time, but that's nerves. Deep down I'm worse than a rabbit."

"What makes you think I'm not the same way?"

"That dress."

Stevi looked down at herself in surprise. "Is something exposed?"

"Honey, the way that dress fits and with your figure, nothing has to be! I just don't know what Dane's going to say when he sees all the men in the place drooling."

"He'd better not say anything," Stevi replied, transferring a few essentials into her small evening bag. "He's the one who asked for this."

Jolene sat down on the arm of the sofa. "Sweet says he heard you practice and told us you were better than Henri."

"I'd remember that right now Henri's not one of Sweet's most favorite people."

"He says that you're almost as good as Miss Dolly Parton."

For a moment Stevi forgot her nerves and her doubts and laughed. Everyone knew that as far as Sweet was concerned, the sun and moon rose and set on Dolly. "I guess I can retire content."

Jolene dropped her gaze to her folded hands. "Sweet seems to admire you a lot."

Hearing the wistfulness in her voice, Stevi was quick to assure her. "Only as a friend. Nothing more. Now, why don't we get going before Dane sends out a search party for both of us?''

He had been sitting at the bar, waiting, when they walked in. She could see it in his eyes as he searched for and spotted her. Thanking Jolene again and excusing herself, she crossed over to him, aware of the way his gaze swept over her to take a detailed inventory of her attire. As usual, he managed to make her forget there was anyone else in the room but him.

''Hi,'' he murmured, as she sat down on the stool beside him.

''Hi.''

''You're nervous.''

''I'm terrified.''

His look was dubious. ''I find that hard to believe. It's obvious this won't be your first opening night.''

''Don't start that again.''

''All right,'' he sighed. ''You look—lovely. Is that better?''

''Much, and thank you.'' She thought he looked good himself; in fact she was surprised at his more formal dress. He wore an off-white linen jacket over a smoke-blue shirt and darker gray slacks. Though he wore no tie and his sleeves were pushed up, the look suited him.

''Can I buy you a drink to settle the butterflies?''

''What butterflies? We're talking whales with wings here.''

Dane smiled, pleased that she hadn't lost her sense of humor despite her reluctance to perform, and signaled Sweet.

''Mercy!'' The burly bartender stared. ''Dane, maybe we should call the riot squad just in case.''

''It crossed my mind.''

"You look real nice, Stevi."

She thanked him and asked him to bring her a sherry. He brought it and moved on to take care of another customer, leaving her alone with Dane again.

"I suppose the routine thing to say in a situation like this would be to wish you luck," he said, lifting his glass in a toast. "Though I still don't happen to think you'll need it."

"But it's nice to hear."

"I wonder if you'd continue to feel that way if I added, thank you for walking through that door two weeks ago."

"Luck of the draw, cowboy; it was the only one in town with a Help Wanted sign."

"What if I added—and into my life?"

Stevi lowered her gaze to avoid being seduced further by the warmth in his eyes. "I might still be flattered, but I think I'd prudently remind you that you shouldn't be saying things like that to me."

"Even though I mean them?"

"*Especially* when you mean them."

"Then if I wanted to play it safe and stay on your good side, I'd do better to stick with the good-luck wishes, wouldn't I?"

Stevi gave in to the smile that tugged at her lips, thinking he must have been irresistible as a child—and devastating once he'd hit his teens. "Sounds like the wisest thing to me."

He touched his glass to hers. "You don't make it easy on a person, Stevi James."

"Well, if it's any consolation, neither do you."

"Good."

His reply was almost a growl, and for a moment Stevi felt a familiar mixture of excitement and nerves she hadn't experienced since she was six years old and her uncle had removed the training wheels from her first bike. But then she also remembered she'd given in to the excitement and had recklessly gone too fast, crashing into Mrs. Joubert's shopping cart and knocking the poor woman down. It had earned her more than a pair of scraped knees.

"On second thought, I'd better go easy on this and warm up my fingers on the piano instead," she said, sliding off the stool.

"Coward."

"That's me. By the way, do you want me to keep time for you the way Henri did? I'm not familiar with the song he played, but I do know a few lines from 'The Eyes of Texas.'"

"No need. I thought I'd spend the evening out here."

"Lucky me," she muttered under her breath.

"That's not going to bother you, is it?"

She wasn't fooled; she knew it pleased him that he'd succeeded in catching her off guard again, and she knew he was aware of the effect his presence would have on her. It had been pretty clear when he'd watched her practice earlier this afternoon. By the time she quit, her insides had been tangled in one huge, complicated knot and she knew there were songs she couldn't possibly play again if he was sitting in the audience. The lyrics would make her feel as though she were having a dialogue directly with him.

But she managed to affect nonchalance with a slight shrug. "You're the boss."

Dane watched her walk away and slowly smiled. *Go ahead,* he thought, *fight it, but it's not going to go away simply because you want it to.* He'd already been able to figure out that much, gauging his own feelings. He *had* fought—who wanted to be attracted to someone who kept backing away from you as though you'd materialized out of their worst nightmare, anyway?—but he'd given up when he realized it wasn't really *him* she was trying to reject but her own feelings.

The way he saw it, that wasn't going to help her much longer. He could see he was getting under her defenses. Her heart was beginning to win some arguments with her head, but it didn't fill him with the cocky satisfaction he might have felt as a younger man. What he felt now was more like relief. He wasn't looking for a conquest. Hell, yes, he wanted her. Just thinking about what it could be like between them made him ache. But whatever this thing was, it went deeper than physical attraction: he cared.

And the timing couldn't be worse.

He reached into the pocket of his jacket and drew out Delia's latest letter, which Sweet had given him this afternoon along with the rest of his mail. There was a time when Dane might have been thrilled to read what she'd written. Now it spawned feelings that were far more complex.

"Problem?" asked Sweet, coming to keep him company for a few moments between orders.

"That's an understatement." Dane sighed and slipped the pink, perfumed envelope back into his pocket. "But I'll manage," he replied, too aware of his friend's opinion of Delia to risk discussing things further.

Across the room Stevi, having completed her warm-up, adjusted the microphone and introduced herself to the audience. Both Dane and Sweet turned their attention to her. It was obvious by the customers' reaction that they were surprised to discover that Henri was gone, but they were also eager to be entertained. Maybe too eager, Dane thought, scowling when he heard the wolf whistles from the back of the room. Then Stevi began to sing, and as he had that afternoon, he forgot everything but the pleasure it gave him to watch her and listen.

"She'll do," Sweet murmured a while later as he went back to his customers.

Dane might have put it more eloquently, but he had to agree: she most definitely would *do*. But what would she say if she suspected he was already contemplating breaking his promise to her about looking for a replacement? Somehow he had to make her understand.

His only hope was that by the time she realized it, she wouldn't care.

Chapter Five

Excuse me, ma'am. Would you care to dance?''

Stevi put down her glass of wine and glanced over her shoulder at the man standing behind her. He was of average height and looks, somewhere in his late thirties or early forties, and indisputably polite. But she still shook her head.

"I don't believe so, thank you."

He blinked as if not sure he'd heard her correctly. "Why not?"

She met Sweet's eyes across the counter, but when he began to reply on her behalf, she signaled discreetly to let him know that she would handle this herself.

"If I agreed to dance with you, then to be fair I'd have to dance with everyone else who asks me, and my breaks aren't that long. I'm sorry."

"Then let me buy you a drink."

"As you can see, I already have a drink."

He appeared to have to think about that a moment before his expression brightened. "Oh, I get it. You're playing hard to get."

This time it was Stevi's turn to blink. She turned back to Sweet and gave him a nod that said "Okay, now it's your turn." He slapped his towel over one big shoulder and leaned across the bar, his usually benign eyes narrowing in warning.

"Mister, far's I can tell, the lady speaks English just fine. She said no, she means no."

The man put up both hands in surrender and backed away.

"Some people," Sweet muttered. "Looks like an out-of-towner."

Stevi lifted a shoulder, ready to dismiss the incident. "Forget it. It happens. Don't tell me you don't have your share of problems keeping the customers straight."

"People liked Henri, but I don't remember them wanting to dance with him."

Smiling, Stevi let the subject drop. She had ten more minutes of her break left and she didn't want to spend it discussing an annoying customer. Taking another sip of her wine she scanned the room. Business was picking up. She could see that in the two days since she'd taken over Henri's job. But instead of feeling proud she was feeling guilty. She'd been hired as a cocktail waitress to make things easier for the others, and it looked as if she were making things worse.

She was also still worried about taking the job in the first place. There was no greater advertisement than word of mouth and the last thing she wanted was for a certain party to discover she was singing here.

"Has Dane had any luck finding someone to replace me yet?" she asked Sweet as he wiped down the section of counter beside her.

"Not that I know."

"If he doesn't do it soon, he's going to have to find another waitress instead. Marge and the others have their hands full—speaking of which, there's Jolene with another order."

Sweet went to take care of her while Stevi watched, casually at first, then with growing interest. For days now she'd suspected there was something going on between them—or trying to. They only had to look at one another to make her believe she was right. They weren't doing much looking now, but that, too, convinced her.

Jolene was doing little more than standing there staring at her tray, her fingernails, or the peanut bowl, while Sweet was suddenly behaving as though he'd never mixed a drink in his life. He had to ask her to repeat her order several times, and even then he ended up giving her the wrong brand of beer.

By the time he returned to Stevi's side of the bar his face was flushed and there were tiny beads of moisture on his forehead. Though he rarely drank, he poured himself a draft beer and wiped his brow with a cocktail napkin.

"Are you going to be okay?" she asked sympathetically.

"I feel like a jerk."

She was tempted to tell him there was a lot of that going around. Running her finger around the rim of her glass, she debated whether it wouldn't be wiser to mind her own business.

"Why don't you ask her out?" she asked impulsively.

He stared at her as if she'd just suggested he climb up on the bar and dance. "Are you kidding? I can't do that," he added, glancing around to make sure no one else was listening.

"Why not? Anyone can see you like each other."

Because of his embarrassment, it took him a moment to realize what she'd said. "You mean you think she likes me *back*?"

"It looks that way from where I'm sitting."

Sweet digested that, but after a moment he still shook his head. "It wouldn't work out."

"Why not?"

"Well, like you said before, she's recently become a widow, and even if the guy wasn't a great husband, I'm not exactly prize material myself. It's true," he insisted, when Stevi gave him a dubious look. "Dane's been good about not ever mentioning it, but I have a reputation for not being reliable that goes way back. Responsibility's never been a strong point with me, and commitment? The only reason I could ever abide the oil rigs was that we were moving all the time. The truth is, coming here and taking on this place is the first time I've ever stuck with someone—and that's only because Dane won't hear of buying me out."

Stevi glanced beyond him across the room to where Dane stood chatting with some customers. It pleased her to know that despite her own need to be cautious, her instincts about the man had been on target.

"That's the strange thing about life, isn't it? Sometimes meeting the right person makes all the difference."

Seeing something in her eyes, Sweet glanced over his shoulder, then frowned. He edged closer to the counter so he could lower his voice. "Uh—Stevi, listen, you and Dane... You're not getting second thoughts about keeping things strictly business, are you?"

"Dane's my boss, Sweet, and hopefully a friend. That's all."

"I just wanted to make sure, because I'd hate to see you get hurt, and I know he's kinda confused these days."

Though she warned herself against it, her curiosity got the best of her. "What do you mean?"

"I think he's still involved in some unfinished business back home."

"At the ranch?"

"Yeah. At the ranch in general. With his sister-in-law, Delia, in particular. See, she was his girl before she dumped him to marry his brother. Only now she can't decide which brother she wants, and I don't think Dane could ever see through that conniving little blonde."

Stevi didn't respond; after all, what was there to say? She'd had to ask and now she knew—more than she wanted. No wonder Dane didn't seem to be involved with anyone here. Who could compete with the memory of a first love, conniving or not?

She gave Sweet a crooked smile and rose. "If I'm not mistaken, that tape you have playing is about to run out. I'd better get back to the piano."

Sweet frowned. "Stevi— Damn. Maybe I should have kept my mouth shut."

"Forget it. I already have."

But as Stevi walked around the bar, she knew that was another lie she was going to have to pay for.

As she was growing up, Stevi remembered one of her aunt's favorite sayings had been about a watched pot never boiling, and she thought of it again as she found herself checking the clock over the bar. But, she decided, as she acknowledged the applause for the latest song she'd completed, she was eager for more than her next break; she was ready to call it a night. Even if she wasn't already emotionally drained, the man who'd made a nuisance of himself earlier would have succeeded in making her feel that way all by himself.

He was sitting at the table nearest the piano. She couldn't see him without turning her head, which she was trying to avoid doing, but she could feel him watching her. By now he could probably recite where every stitch and dart was in her black jumpsuit. Twice now, he'd said something to her. She hadn't heard exactly what, because he'd made his remarks during the applause, but she was certain she didn't care to know.

If only she could get Dane's or Sweet's attention. But the two of them were preoccupied talking to another customer at the bar. She didn't want to create a scene, but she didn't think she could continue playing for much longer, feeling as she did.

She ran her fingers over the black and ivory keys, experimenting with a few chords, and it inspired the memory of another song—and an idea. Raising her head, she looked straight at Dane and began to sing "Someone to Watch Over Me."

Dane felt his waning attention in the conversation severed entirely as he heard Stevi start the song. He'd always liked it; *she* made it into a heartbreaker. Reaching for his drink, he looked up only to find his gaze locked with hers. The rush of pleasure it gave him came quickly and for a moment— No, it was something else. Something was wrong.

He lifted an eyebrow in silent query. Just as subtly, she tilted her head to the right. Dane eyed the dark-haired man sitting alone at the table beside her.

"Sweet," he murmured, right after the man they'd been talking to excused himself and left. "The guy in the blue sport jacket—ever see him before?"

His friend glanced over and made a guttural sound in confirmation. "Penny says he's registered at the motel. I had her find out because he was bothering Stevi a while ago."

"I don't think he's stopped."

He signaled Stevi to take her break and in response she smiled in a way that tempted him to go over and sweep her off the bench himself. As she finished the number and stood up, he did, too. Maybe it was instinct, he told himself; maybe it was an overreaction to the plea he'd seen in her eyes. Either way, it couldn't have been timed better. Just as he reached her, the man at the table took hold of her wrist.

"Let go, mister," Dane said, stopping behind him and speaking so quietly that not even the people at the next table could hear if they'd been paying attention. "Let go or you won't be able to use that hand to lift another drink for a long time."

"I only wanted to invite the lady for a nightcap."

"She's decided to have it with me, and you've decided to leave, preferably without a scene so we won't embarrass her. Got it?"

Dane discreetly escorted the man from the bar and Stevi took advantage of the time to go to the ladies' lounge to freshen up and settle her nerves. When she came back out, Dane had another glass of wine waiting for her.

"Sweet said this is what you're drinking tonight."

"But I don't really want it," she said, although she accepted the bar stool he turned for her.

"Humor me. You look a little pale."

"Yes, doctor."

He smoothed down his moustache. "Don't get cute or I'll give you a hard time for not letting me know sooner that that guy was bothering you."

"I thought I could ignore him. Anyway, thanks for what you did."

"You couldn't have chosen a better song to capture my attention. It's an old favorite of mine."

"Really? Mine, too." Delighted, she turned back to him only to find herself imprisoned by his eyes with a look that went straight to her soul. Oh, why did she have to have met him too late? her heart cried. It would be so easy to fall in love with him. But she mustn't now. Not only was it a luxury she couldn't afford; Sweet had pointed out an equally important reason: he was the wrong man for her.

Dane frowned, sensing her withdrawal as almost a physical thing.

I'm losing you again.

You never had me.

We both know that's not true.

Needing a diversion, Stevi reached for her wine, after all. As she brought it to her lips, the glass clicked lightly against her teeth.

"That might take care of the symptom but not the disease," Dane commented aloud.

In her mind's eye she could picture it—taking two aspirins and in the morning finding this long-legged Texan gone. It made her feel like curling up and crying.

Shaking her head, she firmly set down her glass. "Maybe I'm losing my mind."

"Maybe we both are," Dane amended, although he knew she was really only talking to herself. "Next thing I know, I'll take up flirting with dead-end road signs."

Unfortunately she could picture that, too, and helpless to stop it, Stevi burst into laughter.

The sound, utterly captivating, made Dane's pulse quicken and his blood heat as though he'd just swallowed something far more potent than his bourbon.

"If I were you," he muttered thickly, "I'd start giving thanks."

"I'll bite. What for?"

"Because we're not alone. If we were, you'd pay for that."

"For *laughing*?"

"For sounding so damned sexy you make me ache just listening to you."

Neither of them noticed that Sweet had walked up until he cleared his throat. "Excuse me. Dane, Jerome wants to talk to you about the contract you gave him to repave the parking lot."

"What's there to talk about? He's supposed to start next week."

"Says he can't do it until next month."

That succeeded in causing Dane to tear his gaze from Stevi's. "By then the fall rains will have started and it'll look like a mud-wrestling rink out there." He uttered an oath under his breath and turned back to her. "I'd better go talk to him."

"Good idea."

Rising, he gave her a sidelong look. "Don't sound so pleased. It's just postponing the inevitable."

"That's what you think," she said, grateful she was regaining her senses.

"Going to fight me down to the wire, is that it?"

"One of us has to stay sensible."

About to ask her why, Dane glanced over her bowed head to catch Sweet's disapproving look. He sighed inwardly. His friend was right in what he was obviously thinking. So was Stevi. Dane, with a dozen years' seniority over her—not to mention a lifetime more of experience—was behaving like a teenager chasing his first girl.

He settled for running his finger across her exposed shoulder and took a devilish delight in seeing her shiver. "Sensible it is, then. In that case, why don't you call it an early night and turn in? You've more than earned it."

"But the customers expect—"

"The customers are *my* problem, though I doubt there'll be one. You always give them more than their money's worth, anyway." Grasping her shoulders lightly, he bent closer until his lips brushed her hair. "For once, just do as I ask."

In the end she did—more or less. Although the pleasure she usually took in singing had left her, she knew she was also too tense to sleep; therefore, after leaving the lounge she decided to stroll out front to listen to the night sounds and absorb the sultry night air. As always, she found it soothing.

Across the street she saw Jesse in his usual place. They exchanged waves. She'd taken to visiting with him occasionally, but she hadn't planned on going over there tonight—until she caught sight of a flash of color zipping around the far corner of the building. She followed, curious, and discovered it was indeed Missus, Jesse's cat, looking pleased with herself as she held down a lizard with her paw.

"Got him, did you?" she murmured, crouching to stroke the cat's soft fur. It gave her a friendly mew in greeting and shifted slightly as if to encourage Stevi to inspect her catch. "I know, you still have what it takes. But why aren't you home taking care of the family, hmm? Come on. You don't need that." She lifted the calico cat into her arms. "In a while there'll be cars going every which way out of here. You don't need to get caught in the middle of that, either."

Missus seemed to decide a few minutes of petting outweighed a late-night snack and nestled comfortably against Stevi's breast for the free ride home.

Jesse came outside to greet them. "Early night for you."

"A bit." She handed him the cat. "She's getting tired of playing mother, isn't she?"

"Full moon gives everybody ideas."

Stevi thought back to the incident at O'Neal's. "I guess that's as good a reason as any." She drew a deep breath and wrapped her arms around her waist. Rich scents hung heavily in the air: pine, smoke from a barbecue somewhere, the mysterious musky odor of peat. She'd grown up with them all and they were as comforting as old friends. "Do you think you could learn to live somewhere other than the South, Jesse?"

"Can't say I ever gave it much thought. Reckon not. Not anymore, leastways. I'm old. Be like taking a winter leaf an' sticking it in your pocket to take home. Come time to take it out and it's all busted up. Old things don't travel well."

"Not just old things," Stevi mused sadly. "Things with deep taproots, too."

"Amen to that." He scratched Missus behind her ears. "Think'n about moving on again, are you?"

She didn't want to, but it might come down to where she didn't have a choice. She gave him a sad smile. "Not yet. Anyway, I hear they have full moons everywhere."

"Imagine so."

After wishing him good-night, she recrossed the empty highway. People began to drift out of the lounge. To avoid the possibility of having to strike up a conversation, she circled around the far side of the building. Once she came to the back of the storage shed the scent of roses drew her attention. Guided by the moonlight, she paused to smell the fragrant blossoms before continuing across the lawn.

The man stepped out of the shadow of the pine trees a mere arm's length away. Instinctively she drew back, gasping.

"Shh . . ."

"Louis." Her heart lodged in her throat silencing whatever else she might have said.

He hesitated, then stepped closer. "Who's Louis?"

Moonlight touched him for the first time and she discovered the slicked-back hair was a lighter shade of brown, not black: the facial features were sharp but not as elegant; the eyes were dark but not as cold. He was the man from the lounge.

It seemed insane to feel relieved but she was. "Go away," she demanded, her voice stronger because of it.

"Come on, beautiful, you don't really m-mean that."

Pressing a hand against her thumping heart, she began to step around him. "Yes, I do. And I meant it before, when I said I wasn't interested. Now please go away before I call for help. I don't think you want to have to explain yourself to the police."

He leaned closer and she caught the strong scent of gin on his breath. "W-what's wrong with me? I'm a nice guy." He reached out and grabbed her hand. "C'mon—"

"No!"

Stevi's cry shattered the serenity of the blanketing darkness. An instant later the floodlights from the back of the lounge came on, then she heard an animal's snarl and a man's furious shout. In her panic, her mind seemed to juxtapose which sound came from Dane and which from Bear as both raced toward her from opposite directions.

A whirl of activity followed. The man, jerked backward by Dane, released Stevi and she lost her balance, falling against a pine tree. Through the vertigo and flash of pain that raced up her back, she was only vaguely aware of Dane's fist connecting with the man's jaw or the rending of cloth as Bear took hold of the man's pant leg and yanked. Then Sweet arrived and began trying to separate the two men.

"Dane— Easy, pal. That's enough. Bear! Damn it, dog!" Sweet had to push the dog away with his leg as the animal inadvertently got mixed up and tried to grab hold of his jeans.

"Let me go," Dane warned his friend.

"No way. I'll take him inside and call Lon. We'll let him take the guy in to sleep it off in the parish jail. Tomorrow Stevi can decide whether or not she wants to press charges."

Stevi had crouched down to give Bear an affectionate hug, but when she heard that, she sprang to her feet. "No! He just had too much to drink. As long as he leaves, I'd be willing to forget the whole thing."

While Dane stared at her in disbelief, Sweet hoisted the smaller man to his feet. "Okay, bud. Let's go."

"Are you L-Louis?"

"What? You're nuts."

"Well, *who's* Louis?"

Hearing the exchange, Stevi bit her lower lip and slumped back against the tree before her legs gave out. For a moment she'd been so sure. . . .

"Stevi, are you serious?"

She managed to meet Dane's searching gaze and even attempted a smile. But it took two attempts before she could get her shaking fingers to replace the right shoulder strap of her jumpsuit, which had slipped down. "Yes, of course. Tomorrow, when he sobers up, I'm sure he'll be more than a little embar-embarrassed and—" Feeling the threat of laughter or tears—she wasn't sure which—she pressed her hand against her lips.

She had a feeling she made the initial move to reach out, then Dane was drawing her into his arms and she decided it didn't matter. She wrapped her arms around his neck and held him as if he were her lifeline to sanity.

"When I heard you cry out, I think my heart stopped."

"I feel so silly. He didn't actually scare me."

"I'd have knocked his teeth in if Sweet hadn't stopped me."

"It's probably just fatigue."

Realizing she wasn't listening to a word he said, Dane tucked her closer and simply rocked her back and forth as he would a child. There was something so valiant, and yet so vulnerable about her. She reminded him of a small bird, the kind that bravely chases a hawk from its nest although the hawk is many times larger.

He pressed his cheek against her hair and drew in a deep breath. It was soft. *She* was soft, every sweet inch of her. Never again would he have to lie in bed and imagine what it would be like to feel her against him. Now he could torture himself with other thoughts, like—*Whoa, boy. Just remember why she's in your arms.*

Stevi felt Dane begin to withdraw and tightened her arms. "No, please. Just a moment longer."

Feeling as though he were being ripped in half, Dane pressed his lips to her forehead. "Hush. I'm not going anywhere." When she breathed a sigh of relief he closed his eyes, torn between giving thanks and swearing. "Stevi, what am I going to do about you?"

"I know. I'm more trouble than I'm worth."

Hardly that, but there were discrepancies in her behavior that he couldn't reconcile. How could it be that she could work a room like a professional, keep him at arm's length when he knew she was attracted to him as much as he was attracted to her, and yet fall apart the first time a drunk pushed past the boundaries of good taste?

"Forgive me, but I have to ask even if you don't want to talk about it," he began. "I know you've worked as a singer somewhere before, but I'm having a hard time accepting that this is the first time a guy has tried to come on to you."

"It's because no one would have dared before."

He heard the ice in her voice and knew he'd touched upon something important. "What do you mean 'dared'?"

"The man who owns the place where I used to work had fairly explicit rules. No one was ever to touch what was his—not a piece of furniture or an employee."

"Go on," he murmured, although he wasn't sure he wanted to hear the rest.

Stevi raised her head to look up at him. It was a mistake. They were too close; the night isolated them too well; the look in his eyes mirrored the deepening awareness she felt; and his mouth—

"There *is* nothing else. They just wouldn't have dared, that's all." She dragged her gaze away and slid her hands down to press lightly against his chest. "I think I'm all right now. You can let me go."

"You're not all right. You were scared then, and you're still upset." Dane let go, but only to shift his hold by grasping her upper arms. "Stevi, don't back away from me again—not when you've finally given me something to work with."

"Work with?" Oh, God, she'd never meant to do that! "No!" She pulled herself completely out of his arms. "No," she repeated, less emphatically because she could see what her rejection was doing to him. "You don't realize what you're opening yourself up to. I do. And I won't have it." She ran her hands up and down her arms, suddenly chilled without his protective embrace. "You've been a good friend, Dane. More than I deserve, but I *am* drawing the line here. You have your own...problems to deal with. You don't need the added burden of mine."

"But I *want* to help!"

"Would it stop there?" She shook her head, regret shimmering in her eyes like moonlight on lake water. "Please don't make it harder for me than it already is between us. I like it here, and I'm so tired of being on the road. Make it easier for me to stay."

Dane looked up at the stars and laughed bitterly. "Why not ask me to walk across hot coals while you're at it?"

"You can handle it, cowboy."

Could he? He felt as though he were being split apart from the inside. If anyone had the market cornered on strength, it was she. She reminded him of his mother and the other women he'd known on the ranch where he grew up. Pregnant, sick or simply exhausted, they bore their weight alongside their men, making ends meet, surviving—sometimes out of nothing more than sheer determination. No man he'd ever met proved to be stronger.

He turned back to her, saw how pensively she watched him. Her hair was mussed, her face was as pale as a ghost's, and yet at that moment she was the love-liest sight on earth to him. He was falling for her. That knowledge brought not euphoria, but a deeper ache—and a warped need to reach her somehow, even if it meant using threats.

"I could find out myself, you know. I could have you investigated."

She banked a fleeting wave of panic. "But you won't."

"How can you be sure?"

"I can't. But you can be sure I'd be long gone before you learned anything."

Dane clenched the hands that were back on his hips into fists. Vulnerable? He'd thought she was *vulnerable*? "Remind me never to challenge you to a Mexican standoff, lady," he growled. In frustration he raked a hand through his hair. "Okay—at least you'll let me walk you to your door?"

She did because she wanted to prolong their time to-gether. But the incongruity of her behavior didn't slip by her. What had tempting Providence ever earned anyone besides more trouble? What had happened to the girl who had once indulged in only the simplest dreams of a small house with a vegetable garden out back and a loving husband and children?

"She walked through the wrong door at the wrong time."

"What was that?"

Not realizing that she'd spoken out loud, Stevi glanced around only to discover they were already on the deck where dozens of moths of various shapes and sizes were indulging in their own form of Russian roulette with the floodlights.

"I—um—I said I don't remember putting the key to the door in here," she mumbled, quickly groping in her bag. "Here it is." She managed to get the door unlocked, but then glanced back at him, suddenly feeling awkward. Words of thanks hardly seemed adequate, yet anything more was impossible.

Dane saved the moment by simply brushing her cheek with the backs of his fingers. "Go on. Get some rest if you can. Bear won't leave the area now, and I'll be back as soon as I close up. If you need anything, just pound on the wall."

"Dane—"

"Inside, Stevi. Please."

She went. He waited until she closed the door behind her and he heard the lock set. Then he laid his palm against the outer screen door and waited for the ache to lessen. It didn't.

Chapter Six

They found not a truce—because in actuality there had been no battle—but a median, a status quo by which each day and each exchange was accepted at face value. More than friends and less than lovers, they did nothing to avoid one another—not wanting the rest of their friends to pick up on anything. But their conversations skirted the core of their feelings as carefully as those of two diplomats testing the uncharted waters of a détente.

Dane hated it. However, considering the options open to him, he found it the lesser of evils. At least he could find comfort in knowing that she wanted to stay. It made him repress the second thoughts he'd had about calling her bluff and phoning Lon Bolton, the parish sheriff, after all, to see what he could dig up on her. Given time, he decided, another solution might present itself, or he might succeed in breaking down those walls of secrecy she kept around herself and convince her to confide in him.

In the meantime he nursed his frustrations by watching her perform every night and mollified himself somewhat by keeping a careful eye on his customers to make sure that history didn't repeat itself. Even so, the days seemed to take forever to get through. And the nights...

Who was Stevi, really? At night, in his bed, that question returned to haunt him again and again. Oh, she was a treasure, all right; but he'd always been leery of windfalls. Everything he had, had come from hard work. Pride made him prefer it that way. Why, then, he wondered, had she walked through *his* front door? And what was her secret? At this point, all he knew was that she was running from something or *someone*. Of that he was certain. He had a feeling it had to do with where she'd worked before; her ex-boss didn't sound like the type of guy he would want to get to know on a personal level. Was he somehow behind all this? Or was Stevi running because of something *she* had done?

No. His gut instincts rejected that idea. Only a person with a conscience would insist on protecting outsiders. But he couldn't help worrying that as a result, she was making herself even more vulnerable; the rule that there was safety in numbers might apply on more than one level here. The question was, *did* it? Until she decided to trust him, he wasn't going to know.

On Wednesday morning he woke to the weatherman's report on the radio and the promise of rain, but when he went outside a while later, he found the same cerulean blue sky and glaring sun that had greeted him for the past several days. It was just as well, he told himself. He wanted to go to Mooringsport to pick up a few things anyway, and driving on oil-slick roads wasn't his idea of the best way to do it.

First, however, he went to his office to catch up on some paperwork. As much as he enjoyed listening to Stevi, she was turning his schedule upside down—a problem, he noted dryly, he had never suffered from with Henri.

It was late morning when he emerged outside again, and the sky was no longer blue but covered by heavy gray clouds. While standing under the breezeway debating whether he should postpone his trip for another day, he glanced through the glass door of the café and spotted Stevi talking to Chloe, one of the newer waitresses. The two of them were making the strangest hand signals. Intrigued, he went inside.

"Let me guess," he drawled, admiring the mint-green blouse and matching slacks Stevi was wearing. "Chloe's teaching you the Indian song her kids learned at day camp."

Stevi dropped her head back and groaned at the ceiling, wondering if she could do *anything* around here without his finding out. "Close. She's teaching me how to shift."

Dane hesitated, a dozen and one responses coming to mind, none of which—he was sure—she would appreciate. "Shift what?" was the bland though safer course he chose to take.

"My VW," Chloe told him, gesturing to the paintless wonder parked out front. "She needs to run some errands and I offered her the use of my car—it's not like she can hurt it, right?—but she can't shift."

"No problem. She can ride with me. I was about to go to town myself."

The look Stevi tossed him was more censuring than grateful. "How can I refuse an offer like that?"

"You can't." He plucked Chloe's car keys out of Stevi's grasp, and with a wink, tossed them to the waitress. "Shall we go?"

Once outside, Stevi stopped, despite the hand he had at the small of her back urging her along. "Were you really going?"

"How often do you see me in anything but jeans and a T-shirt before the lounge opens?" he asked, extending his arms to invite her scrutiny.

She reluctantly took in his blue shirt and tan slacks, not wanting to be reminded that he looked wonderful in work clothes, and if possible, even more so now. The light blue complemented his tan, and the fit of the slacks couldn't have been better if they'd been tailored.

"I can't say I give it a great deal of thought."

He feigned a narrow-eyed look, and taking her elbow, led her to his black pickup truck. "Go ahead, try to convince yourself you're not relieved you don't have to drive in that rusted sardine can. Or that you're not secretly pleased to have me along for company," he added, holding the door for her as she climbed in.

"I suppose you *would* come in handy in case of a flat tire."

In reply he slammed the door and circled the front of the truck to get in beside her. "Aren't you in rare form today."

"Yes, as a matter of fact I am." But she wasn't going to let him know that it was because she was having second thoughts and really *was* glad he was taking her.

As Dane started the motor and pulled out onto the road, Stevi waved to Jesse, who was pumping gas, and settled back to enjoy the ride. Cloudy or not, this was scenic country, and the vegetation was lush and varied. "It looks like we're going to have another good muscadine crop this year," she murmured, noting a particularly laden vine climbing along a half-fallen tree. "When I was little, my aunt used to make muscadine jam every year. One Sunday after church we'd drive out to her favorite spot—an abandoned farm with a dilapidated barbed-wire fence drenched in vines—and she, my uncle and I would pick grapes all afternoon. Then for the next several evenings we would congregate around the kitchen table and pluck grapes off the stems to get them ready for boiling. Well, just my aunt and I; my uncle kept us company playing his harmonica."

"I always did like the sound of one. Was he any good?"

"My aunt said he sounded like an old tomcat dragging himself home after a rough night, but I thought he was wonderful. My favorite songs were the ones he played about the railroad. He used to be a railroad man in Lake Charles before he hurt his hip in an accident."

It was on the tip of his tongue to ask her if that was where she was originally from, but Dane decided not to risk having her clam up again. "Was the jam good?" he asked instead.

"Yes, though it was difficult to justify the amount of time and labor that went into it as opposed to what you can pick up on a market shelf. I suppose you have to count companionship as part of the yield." She cast him an impish look. "I'll tell you what tasted better—the homemade wine my uncle made every year from his own private stock of grapes. He did it in his old toolshed out back and I used to help him. It was my job to get the sugar from the local grocery store. He said if he went, everyone in the parish would know what he was up to."

Dane chuckled and asked, "Did your aunt ever catch him?"

"Eventually. But before that I almost blew it for him by sneaking into the shed after school one day and sampling what to me seemed no different from the grape juice they served during Communion at church." Stevi touched her fingers to her lips, her eyes bright with laughter. "I was ten years old. When I walked into the kitchen for dinner that evening singing 'That Old Black Magic,' I thought my uncle was going to suffer apoplexy. He told me later that I did him a favor by passing out over my crawfish étouffée before my aunt could discover what was wrong. He was able to convince her that it must have been a fever I picked up at school.

"But she finally caught on to him two years later. We had a particularly hot summer, like this one has been, and it dragged into fall. My uncle's brew began to ferment too fast and one day the glass jugs began exploding. My aunt was out back hanging the wash. She ran into the house screaming that crazy old Antoine Joubert—who was rather famous for being the worst poacher in the parish—was headed this way trying to track a deer or wild pig he'd winged. My poor uncle tried his best to keep her inside after things calmed down, but she was determined to go next door and give old Antoine a piece of her mind."

"What happened?" Dane demanded, taking his eyes off the road long enough to see Stevi wiping tears from the corners of her eyes.

"My uncle and I stayed where we were, sitting at the kitchen table staring at one another in helpless horror. I think I'll remember the way his Adam's apple kept bobbing up and down until the day I die. Suddenly there was this unholy scream from outside and my uncle just dropped his head down onto his folded arms and began moaning. You see, when the glass jugs exploded, they broke through the window in the shed and as my aunt passed her clothesline, she saw her wash just dripping with the remains of my uncle's homemade wine.''

''I'll bet your uncle was in the doghouse for a while after that,'' Dane said after he stopped laughing.

''And how. He wasn't allowed to miss another Sunday church service for months.''

Stevi sighed and looked out the passenger window.

''What are you thinking now?''

''How long ago all that seems. I didn't realize until years later that my uncle had a drinking problem. It finally killed him. My aunt seemed to lose interest in life after that.'' She glanced at Dane. ''It's strange the way relationships work. I'd never thought of them as particularly close, they were simply *married*.''

''I know what you mean. My parents weren't demonstrative, either. But after my mother passed away, I remember once suggesting to my father that he join the rest of us who were going to the local dance hall. He declined, saying he'd been married to the only woman he ever wanted and that we should go on and not worry about him.''

''How sweet . . . and sad.''

''I carry a picture of them in my—oh, hell,'' he muttered, grabbing at his right hip.

''What's wrong?''

''My wallet. I think I forgot my wallet.''

''I don't believe it. *You* actually forgot something?''

''It's on my desk. I'd been looking for a business card because I needed a phone number,'' he explained, slowing down.

"Usually you're giving Sweet a hard time for being the absentminded one."

"This has nothing to do with being—" The road was too narrow to make a clean turn and the truck rocked wildly as Dane steered off the pavement onto the lower, gravel shoulder, and back on again. "Sorry about that."

"They're not *my* tires taking a beating."

"Bite your tongue. These things barely have ten thousand miles on them."

"Nails and glass being inanimate objects, they probably don't suffer from prejudice."

"Cute. Where were we? Oh, yeah—Sweet."

"By the way, where is he today? I haven't seen him yet and he's usually around by late morning."

"He called and said he'd be late. There was something he wanted to do. Worried about him?"

"I'm concerned for all the people I work with," she insisted.

"Does that include me?"

Him most of all, but she would be out of her mind to admit that. She laced her hands primly over the purse on her lap and kept her gaze on the road before them. "Don't look now but you're starting to get obvious."

"Maybe I should have let you tackle Chloe's minitank, after all."

"Well, since we're headed back in that direction, it can still be arranged."

"Sure, and halfway to Mooringsport you'd have a breakdown. The only reason Chloe still drives that thing is because she lives just three miles from the café. Forget I said anything. At least this way I know you'll get where you're go-ing. Oh, for crying out loud."

Seconds after the thumping sound began in the front of the truck it was joined by a rhythmic lurching. Dane uttered a low growl under his breath and pulled over. The flat tire made the passenger side of the cab tilt to the right and Stevi leaned to the left trying desperately to sit up and hold back the grin that was pulling at the corners of her mouth.

"Not a word," Dane warned.

"I'll do my best." He reached for the door handle. "Need any help?"

If she didn't know him better, she might have been intimidated by the look he shot her. Instead, she got out on her side, and when he came around the front, they observed the flat tire together.

"It's probably a nail," she murmured, clasping her hands behind her and rocking back and forth on her heels. "I didn't see any glass around where we turned."

"Thank you, Doctor Watson."

Dane began jerking his shirt out of his pants, then unbuttoning it. What next? he fumed. All he'd done was take advantage of the opportunity to spend a few hours alone with her. Did that warrant being hounded by the black cloud that was obviously hanging over his head? Sighing, he hung his shirt on the sideview mirror and went to get the jack and tools he needed from the toolbox in the bed of the truck.

Stevi was grateful for the distance that put between them, but still watched him out of the corner of her eye. She couldn't help it; his body intrigued her. She liked the powerful yet sleek lengths of muscle stretched along bone. And that wedge of hair that covered his chest . . . It was almost black and would feel, she decided, a little ticklish, slightly rough to the touch, the way his mustache did when he kissed her on the forehead. She slid her hands into the pockets of her slacks to counter the urge to test that theory and turned away under the pretense of looking around.

This wouldn't do at all, she thought, lifting her damp hair off the back of her neck. It wasn't the first time she would watch a bare-chested man working.

"Hey, don't wander too far off!"

She turned on her heel, lifted a hand in acknowledgement, but continued walking.

Well, not just *any* bare-chested man, she mused, watching him crouch to slide the jack under the truck. Certainly none that had ever made her feel this... restless. She pivoted on her heel again.

She had come closest with Paul; had believed, even hoped that he would be the one to make her come alive and feel those things that before she'd only sung about in songs. But there was no forcing something out of what was never meant to be. How ironic that when she finally did meet that special man, the timing couldn't be worse.

Kicking one of last season's pinecones out of her way, she wondered what Delia Randolph looked like. Probably petite, limpid eyed and all-around gorgeous. She couldn't resist hoping the woman got everything she deserved, and she *didn't* mean Dane!

After a while a threatening roll of thunder rumbled in the distance. She glanced up at the sky. "You wouldn't...?"

In reply a fat raindrop landed on her nose.

"Dane! Hurry! It's about to—" Before she could finish, the skies opened up to a torrential downpour. She was drenched before she was halfway back to the truck. What next? she wondered, beginning to give in to the lunacy of it all by laughing.

"Cut it out," Dane sputtered, rolling the flat and hoisting it into the bed of the truck. "You think this is funny?"

She scooped up his wrenches for him and dropped them into the toolbox. "Well, don't *you*?"

"Yeah, I guess so," he replied, beginning to grin. "It's either that or cry."

"Aw—" She plucked his shirt from the mirror and handed it to him. "Look at it this way, at least this didn't get dirty."

"Great. Just great."

But he gave in to her contagious humor and they stood there on that desolate roadway until her clothes, heavy with water, clung to her body like another layer of skin, and rivulets ran in geometric patterns down his chest.

Which one of them stopped laughing first? she wondered.

When did the sparkles in her eyes turn to awareness? he asked himself.

Dane looked down at his hands and frowned.

"What is it?"

"They're dirty."

"Of course, they're dirty; you just changed a flat."

"But I want to touch you." He wiped them as best he could into his shirt and flung it through the open passenger window.

"Wait a minute." Stevi took a backward step, only to find herself against the side of the truck. "Dane, this isn't a good idea."

He blocked her path by placing his left hand against the truck and snaking his right one around her waist. "That's not what your eyes said. Your eyes said yes."

Stevi closed them and in her mind hunted for some small corner of sanity to cling to. More thunder rumbled and the rain fell even faster and harder. They were either going to be struck dead where they stood by lightning, Stevi thought, get washed away by a flash flood—or she was going to die of exquisite torture from the pleasure of feeling his body pressed against hers. But this wasn't supposed to be happening. He had no right. As he began to sip raindrops from her eyelids, her cheeks and chin, a small whimper of protest broke from her lips.

"Damn you, Dane Randolph."

"Don't talk, love," he whispered against her lips. "Just kiss me."

He crushed his mouth against hers, not cruelly, but with a hunger that would tolerate no denial. And yes, she discovered, his mustache *did* tickle for a moment— only as long as it would take a lit match to turn a stack of hay into an inferno. Stevi felt the heat scorch every inch of her body, and sliding the hands she'd been pushing against his chest up around his neck, she melted against him.

Once, she pleaded with her conscience, *let me have this one moment to know what it could have been like.* Never had a kiss moved her so quickly, this deeply. She slid her fingers into the drenched hair curling at his nape and blissfully returned all the passion and pleasure he was giving her. It felt so perfect, he felt so strong; she wanted to touch him, explore him, but she didn't want to give up, even for a moment, the wonderful sensation of feeling her breasts crushed against his chest.

He slid his hands over her back, molding her closer, and brushed the outer swell of one breast with his fingertips. It sent a thrilling current through her that left

her trembling against him and had him muttering
something indecipherable and pressing his mouth to her
throat.

They weren't aware of the approaching truck until the
giant timber hauler actually roared past them, the driver
facetiously giving them a blast of his horn. Shock gave
Stevi the strength to push Dane away. He sent the man
an evil look, before trying to reassure her.

"Sweetheart, he was only being a wise guy."

Hardly paying attention, she covered her face with
her hands. "Oh, God, I don't believe what I've just
done, what I let you do."

"Why don't we get into the truck?" he suggested,
folding her into his arms again. "If we try hard enough,
we might even be able to steam up the windows and
have a little privacy." He expected her to laugh softly or
at least give him a sheepish look from under those
adorable lashes, but what he got was an indignant cry
and a quick shove.

"At least *I*'m honest enough to admit this was a mistake and willing to shoulder my share of the blame, but
you— I suppose you're capable of simply closing your
eyes because one woman's no different from another,
is that it?"

"What are you talking about?"

"I'm telling you!"

"Well, I don't get it!"

"Please don't make this any more difficult than it has
to be," she said, turning to reach for the door.

"Difficult?" Dane swung her back into his arms with
a force that left her plastered to him from breast to
thigh. "It doesn't get any more difficult than *this*. What
happened to the woman I was just kissing a minute ago,
the one who was kissing me back and trembling be-

cause she wanted it, wanted *me*?'' When he began to lower his head to kiss her, she evaded him by turning away, and his eyes mirrored both disbelief and hurt. ''I want you, Stevi. I wanted you from the moment you walked into my office. How much more honest can I get?''

''Try admitting that if we would make the mistake of letting this go too far, I'd only be a substitute for another woman.''

All emotion drained from his face and he slowly released her. For the space of a few heartbeats they stood there with the rain continuing to pound down on them, their eyes locked in silent battle. Then Dane curtly told her to get into the truck and he went to collect the rest of his tools.

Stevi had always known that there had to be a tougher, colder side to the man who'd charmed her; a side that would make it possible for him to boss any steer that tried to boss him, and to survive the elements and heaven only knew what else out on those overseas oil rigs. She had a feeling she was about to get an introduction to that man, and even though she couldn't completely blame him for what he might be thinking of her now, she wasn't looking forward to this.

When he climbed in on the driver's side, he reached for his shirt and wiped his face with the cleanest section. Afterward, while turning to study her profile, he rubbed what moisture he could from his chest. ''Now. Why don't you tell me what that crack was all about.''

She had taken a brush from her purse, but when she heard the restraint in his low voice, her hands began to tremble and she settled for clutching it between them as she would a life preserver. ''Dane, I didn't mean to be cruel.''

"What did you mean to be?"

She bowed her head, accepting his sarcasm. "You're right; I wanted you to kiss me, and I am attracted to you. But I had no business giving in to those feelings, and for that matter neither did you, because you have your own problems—"

"That's the second time you've said that. What problem? *What other woman?*"

Stevi took a deep breath and exhaled. "I know about Texas and the ties you still have to the ranch."

"You've already lost me. I told you, my brother runs the place now. I'm completely out of it."

"Ties to your sister-in-law."

His mouth flattened into a hard line. "I think you've been talking with Sweet."

"He was only trying to help. Both of us."

"He was sticking his nose into something he knows nothing about. And I'll tell you something else, lady; discovering you *think* I'd be capable of the things you're suggesting is just as bad as being guilty of them. You were right about one thing, though; what happened outside was one big mistake.

"I have a news flash for both of you," he continued, half turning in his seat. "One: I have never, and would never, use one woman to forget another. Two: that business about Texas is garbage. Sure, Delia and I once had something going, and yes, I was hot under the collar when she broke off with me to take up with Clay. But that's history. As competitive as we might be as siblings, he's still family. I'd never try to take his wife away from him. Maybe I was a bit slow in picking up what's been behind all those letters my pretty but spoiled sister-in-law has been sending me, or maybe I've just tried to turn a blind eye in the hope that I'm wrong about her, but if she thinks I'm her escape route out of a bad marriage, she has a big surprise coming.

"When I kissed you a few minutes ago, I kissed *you*—or at least the woman I thought you were. But it's obvious she doesn't exist. Whatever problems you *think* you have, you're welcome to them. They're probably as mythical as the one you fabricated for me."

Moving around to face front, he turned the ignition key and started the motor, then the windshield wipers. When he shifted into drive, the truck jerked and the tires spun on the wet pavement from his rough handling.

They completed the drive back to O'Neal's in silence. Stevi decided it was just as well; for most of the trip she had enough to deal with, trying to blink back the tears that kept flooding her eyes. When they were finally parked in front of the lounge, Dane yanked the keys out of the ignition but hesitated as he reached for the door handle.

"I'm going upstairs to change before leaving for Mooringsport again. You'll understand if I prefer to make this next trip alone."

"Of course," Stevi murmured, although he was already half out of the truck. On impulse she hurried after him. "Dane?"

He paused at the far end of the breezeway—paused, but refused to turn around. "What?"

"I just wanted to let you know— I'll pack my things and be sure to catch the evening bus."

"You do and you'll find out what real problems are," he growled, spinning around and pointing a finger level with her nose. "We have a contract, lady. It might not be in writing, but a deal is a deal. You'll play in the lounge until I can find someone else, and if you try to sneak off, I'll come after you. So help me, I will. Got it?''

Stevi stared at him in horror, unable to believe what she was hearing.

"I said, got it?"

She tried to answer but the words wouldn't come. In the end she gave him the answer he was waiting for by simply nodding.

Later, after she was sure he was gone and she had showered and changed herself, Stevi went down to the lounge to practice, hoping she might find some small comfort in her music. Sweet was there and it was obvious that he was in a much happier frame of mind.

"Am I glad to see you," he told her, pausing from sorting the mail. "You're never going to guess—she said yes!"

Stevi went straight to the piano and sat down, though she usually joined him at the bar for a few minutes. "Who said yes?"

"Jolene. She said she'd go out with me!"

"Oh...that's great. That's really wonderful, Sweet. I'm very happy for you."

"Thanks. If it wasn't for you, I might never have built up the nerve. Hey, are you all right? You look kind of—oh-oh. I hear a delivery truck headed around the back. Later," he promised, disappearing through the stockroom door.

Not if I can help it, Stevi thought, running through a few chords. She was going to pull herself together. She wasn't going to cry on anyone's shoulder. After all, what for? She'd wanted Dane to leave her alone and now she was going to have her wish. What more could she ask for?

Jolene and Sweet... That was nice. At least it looked as if things were working out for them.

She was halfway through the old Gershwin tune, "But Not For Me," before she realized what she was playing and abruptly snatched back her hands.

Two minutes later when Sweet returned, eager to tell her of his plans, Stevi was gone.

Chapter Seven

"Where's Dane hiding himself these days?"

Stevi looked up from the drink she was having with the middle-aged couple who were regulars at the lounge and shrugged, though inside her heart felt weighed down. "I guess he stays busy in his office, Mr. Frankston. Being a businessman yourself, you know what it's like."

"I know if you give too much of yourself to it, it can kill you. That's why after my bypass surgery I made a point of taking a night or two off every week to enjoy life with Molly, here." Through bifocals he winked at the matronly woman beside him who was happily sipping her frozen margarita.

"Well, I'm only one of the hired help," Stevi replied, adding a smile to soften the effect of her words. "And I suppose as long as he doesn't tell me what songs to sing, I should let him work the hours he wants to." She slid her empty wineglass toward the center of the table, signaling her impending departure, and rose. "Thank you so much for the drink, but if I don't go check on my hair and makeup now, I'll be late starting my next set."

"Thank *you*," Molly said in a hushed voice. "Why, you're the first celebrity we've ever had a chance to buy a drink for!"

"Celebrity... Oh, dear. Bless you." Stevi waved and made her way through the rest of the tables and past the bar toward the ladies' lounge. *Celebrity.* How little it took to please some people, and how grateful she was that they had accepted her explanation of Dane's absence these past several days.

Since their scene last Wednesday, it had been painfully obvious to her why he'd been making himself scarce lately. He was avoiding her, even at the cost of neglecting his own customers. From the time they opened till closing, he locked himself behind that solid oak door to his office, rarely coming out, and then only to ask Sweet something or go into the back storeroom to check stock against invoices. It hurt. But it also annoyed her. If it bothered him to have her around, why didn't he make things more pleasant for both of them and release her from their agreement? Did he think it was worth disappointing his patrons? The regulars enjoyed the personal attention they had come to know they could expect here; it was one of the reasons why, in the past ten days, she had made an effort to compensate for his absence and visit with some of the customers herself, despite her instinct to maintain a lower profile and just do her job. In his anger toward her he was thinking only of himself; he forgot that there were Sweet, Marge and the others who relied on him to keep things running smoothly.

"Men!" she muttered for the second time that month as she stepped into the ladies' lounge.

"Yeah, aren't they great?" Jolene replied, pausing in the act of carefully relining her lips to grin at her in the wide mirror.

Beside her, Marge rolled her eyes and dropped her cigarette case and lighter back into her purse. "How quickly she forgets. How's it going, kiddo? Any sign of life from the great beyond?"

Stevi shook her head.

"And you still don't want to talk about it?"

"There's nothing to talk about." Stevi tried to redirect attention from herself to Jolene. "You certainly are in a good mood these days. I take it things are continuing to go well between you and Sweet?"

"I hate people who think they invented romance," Marge said before the other woman could reply. She tucked her purse under her arm. "My sixteen-year-old is the same way. Last month he was still my sweet, conniving garbage collector who thought girls were a disease transmitted through any contact with soap and water. This month a cute little girl moved in next door and suddenly I can't get *into* my bathroom because he's locked himself in there while he hunts for peach fuzz to shave off his chin. And now, whenever I open my mouth, it's 'Mother, you don't understand.' *Mother*. God, I feel old." Still rambling, she walked out.

Stevi and Jolene exchanged looks in the vanity mirror and burst into laughter.

"She's been like that all evening," Jolene told her, closing her lip brush and compact. "It's scary to think I may go through the same thing with Sean and Joey one day."

"I wouldn't start worrying yet. After all, they're only seven and four, right? Instead, why don't you tell me what's put all those new stars in your eyes—as if I needed to ask."

Jolene blushed, causing her freckles to almost disappear. "It's Sweet. He's so..."

"Sweet?"

"Yeah. Does that sound corny to you?"

"Not if it's true."

Jolene watched Stevi brush on another stroke of blusher over each cheekbone to replace what had worn off and to tone down the shine that the heat from the overhead lights created. "You know, even before I knew I liked you, I was jealous." Seeing Stevi pause in midstroke and eye her skeptically, she nodded. "It's true. Everyone thinks blondes get all the attention, but next to you I'm like cotton candy, while you're mysterious and sexy."

Feeling a little uncomfortable, Stevi opted to try to make a joke out of the situation. "How does a snubnosed vagabond like me qualify as mysterious?"

"It's your whole *aura*, I think the word is. It's the way you move—you don't walk, you glide."

"Something like a snake, huh?"

"I'm serious. And when you look at people, it's always from underneath those lashes that I'd give my favorite Elvis tape for. Kind of cautious. Everything about you is warm but cautious. It makes a person wonder."

"I'm glad I'm able to provide so much entertainment," Stevi drawled, replacing her blusher in her cosmetic bag and taking out her navy eyeliner. Feeling the slight unsteadiness in her fingers, she tossed it back and settled for her hairbrush.

"Oh, everyone respects your privacy, Stevi, but you can't stop people from fantasizing. What else do they have to do out here? And just looking into your eyes, anyone knows you've seen things and have been hurt. Sweet and I were talking the other day and we decided you're running away from a man you loved but who was cruel to you, and that the reason you don't like to talk about your past is because he's filthy rich and has hired an entire detective agency to find you and bring you back."

Luckily Stevi had bent at the waist and was brushing her hair forward, hiding her face. It gave her the time she needed to collect herself.

"Close," she said, straightening and tossing her hair back to brush it into place. "But it's my father who's filthy rich, and I'm running away from him because he wants me to marry an Arab sheikh business associate of his who already has *four* wives. But I'm telling you this in strict confidence. For all I know, Daddy has already put out a reward on me."

Wide-eyed, Jolene stared at her for several seconds, wondering if she was serious or teasing. Finally she grimaced and dismissed the story with a wave. "Go ahead and make jokes, but we'll stick with our theory."

"I would think that you and Sweet would have more interesting things to talk about, not to mention *do*, than waste time conjuring up adventures about me."

"There's time for that, too," Jolene admitted, glancing demurely at her from beneath her own cinnamon-brown lashes. "Haven't he and Dane led the most interesting lives?"

"From what little I've learned, I'd say so."

"When I first came to work at the café six months ago, he scared me to death. Now I can't imagine why I ever thought that. He's the most gentle man. The boys are already crazy about him. He took us to a carnival in Shreveport after church last Sunday. It was a first for Sean and Joey. They literally wore themselves out on the rides and games; and when it came time to walk back to the truck, Sweet hoisted one on each shoulder and carried them like sacks of feed. They thought that was the best ride of all.''

Stevi could picture the scene and understood the twinge of envy she felt. ''I'm glad to hear that Joey has gotten over his initial fear of Sweet.''

''Has he ever.'' Jolene laughed wryly, running a hand over her sleeveless turquoise sweater and matching slacks. ''We're lucky to find whatever time we can to be alone.''

As Stevi adjusted the black ribbon at the low collar of her poet's shirt and brushed away a piece of lint from her black satin slacks, she did some quick decision making. ''You know if you ever need someone to keep the boys, even overnight, I'd be happy to. I know you told me your mother watches them while you're here, but maybe she wouldn't mind the break, either.''

''Do you mean it? Oh, that would be wonderful. Sweet had asked me if I wanted to take in a movie someplace and maybe a late-night dinner Sunday, but since it's Labor Day weekend Mama has to work extra hours at the market. This would give us both a break. Are you sure?''

''Positive. Let me know what you decide, and now we'd both better get out there before somebody sends a search party for us.''

They exchanged greetings with the two women who came through the door as they were leaving and halfway down the hall almost bumped into Dane, who was making a selection at the cigarette machine.

"I didn't know you smoked," Stevi blurted out before she could think to stop herself.

He straightened and looked, she thought for a moment, guilty. Then his eyes turned cool and censuring. "You have your secrets, I have mine. Aren't you supposed to be working, or are you attempting to match Henri's record for prolonged breaks?"

"I was about to go back on."

"See that you do," he snapped back just as edgily. Turning on his heel, he walked off.

When he was out of earshot, Jolene touched Stevi's shoulder. "What's going *on* between you two? A few weeks ago we were all speculating there might be something serious developing, but now we're ducking to avoid getting frostbite."

"That's the way things go."

"Can I help?"

Stevi reached up and gave the hand on her shoulder a pat to assure her she was all right. "Yes. Have Sean and Joey stay with me over the holiday weekend. It'll help keep me preoccupied."

Jolene took Stevi up on her offer and on the following Sunday, right after breakfast, she and Sweet brought the boys over. They had met Stevi before and had seemed to like her well enough, but as their mother kissed them goodbye, it was clear that they thought they were being abandoned.

"Why can't we go with you and Sweet?" Joey asked, obviously not for the first time, if Jolene's weary expression was anything to go by.

"Hey wait a minute," Stevi said to the smaller boy, who was a miniature version of his mother. "You're going to give me a complex."

"What's a complex?"

"Zucchini brain," his elder brother muttered. He was dark-haired as his father had been, and one day he would stand head and shoulders above his mother, but the eyes he would break hearts with were very much Jolene's.

"I only meant that you're going to make me feel bad because I have lots of fun things planned for us to do," Stevi said before Jolene could reprimand either of them.

Still pouting, Joey gave her a doubtful look. "What kind of things?"

"Well, I need two talented young men to help me paint the storage shed for Sweet...."

"That's not fun, that's work," Sean grumbled.

"It can be fun work—and," she added, playing her trump card, "it pays fairly well. If I'm not mistaken, your mother said you needed to earn some spending money for the state fair Sweet has promised to take you to."

"Hey, yeah!" the boys cried in unison.

"I guess that settles that," Sweet drawled, after Stevi told the boys where to put their overnight bags and gave them permission to start getting the paint out of the storage shed. "We really appreciate this, Stevi."

"Especially taking them even earlier than we discussed," Jolene added.

"My pleasure," Stevi assured them. "But maybe you'd better wait to thank me until after you see what they do to their clothes."

"I told Dane about the boys being here and the shed," Sweet told her, keeping his voice low and glanc-

ing toward his friend's window as though he expected
to see him there at any moment. When she thanked him
and asked him what Dane's reaction had been, Sweet
hung his head and looked like a man with split loyal-
ties. ''Well, I won't say he was thrilled, at first, but after a few days he asked me if I was sure you had enough
paint, and to remember to get those rosebushes trimmed
back as I'd promised. It's obvious he doesn't want to see
anyone get hurt.''

It was another example of Dane's inner conflict over
how to react to her, Stevi thought, wishing he would
make up his mind one way or another, and soon. It was
getting to her, too. After that scene by the cigarette
machine, he'd once again done his disappearing act. But
two days later, when he came upon her carrying a small
stepladder up the deck stairs because she had to replace
a burned-out light-bulb, he'd insisted on doing it for her
and then had lingered afterward, asking if there were
any other things that needed repair or replacing. But
then yesterday, when she'd forgotten to give him a
phone message, he'd snapped at her.

''We'll manage,'' she assured Jolene and Sweet,
gently nudging them back down the deck stairs. ''You
concentrate on having a good time and don't worry
about coming back until you're ready to.''

Following them, she was almost at eye level with the
deck when something made her look up and glance into
Dane's kitchen window, only to find him sitting at the
table, Sunday paper in one hand and a mug of coffee in
the other. But he wasn't reading, he was looking at her.
The contact only lasted a second or two; still, she was
glad she had one hand on the railing. It only took that
long for him to unsettle her and force her to look down
to locate the step where she should place her foot.

Had he been listening to them? Had she said anything that might embarrass herself one way or another? Why didn't he come out and say goodbye to
Sweet and Jolene? She knew he approved of the rela-
tionship. This whole situation was getting to be too
much. How much longer was he going to let it continue
before he did them both a favor and located someone to
take her place? Maybe she should ask Sweet about it
before he left? No, why bring up the subject and put a
damper on his day. She would ask Dane himself—right
after she had built up enough nerve.

Dane watched them on and off for the next hour in
between finishing his newspaper and cleaning up the
breakfast dishes. Even Bear had decided the laughing
and singing were irresistible and had let himself out to
join them. Now woman, boys and dog had almost as
much paint on themselves as they had on the shed. Dane
wished he had, too. Jolene had nice kids—polite, but
with a healthy streak of mischievousness in them. Yet,
they weren't the real reason why he wanted to be included in the fun; he wanted to be with Stevi. It was the
one conclusion he'd come to. The rest—his feelings over
what she thought him capable of and his disappoint-
ment that she couldn't trust him enough to confide in
him—when weighed against it, didn't change anything. He'd tried to stay annoyed with her; he couldn't.
He'd tried to ignore her; he couldn't. It was time to do
something, but what?

Outside, Joey was insisting that it was his turn to
climb the ladder and paint the upper portion of the
shed. Dane watched Stevi patiently bargain with his
brother until Sean grudgingly agreed. Triumphant, Joey
dipped his brush, then began his cautious climb, while

a steady stream of white paint saturated the bedsheets covering the rosebushes. Once on top, the youngster made two wild sweeps with his brush, decided he needed more paint, and began to descend.

Holding the ladder, Sean groaned and dropped his head onto his arm, Stevi turned away to try to suppress a grin, and Joey stepped off the last rung—straight into the paint bucket.

When opportunity presented itself, Dane thought, heading for the door, only a fool ignored it.

"I didn't see it, Stevi. Honest."

"I know, sweetheart, but if you keep that up, we're not going to have enough paint to finish the job." Stevi brushed the back of her hand across her itchy forehead and tried hard not to give in to the laughter that was beginning to choke her. "What on earth are we going to do with you now?"

"Use him as a brush," suggested Sean, thoroughly disgusted with his younger brother.

"Uh-uh!"

"Shh! Boys, have a heart," Stevi said, her voice urgent and low. "If Dane sees this mess, he's going to have a fit. Joey, stay where you are and I'll go get another sheet for you to step onto so you don't turn the grass—oh!" Turning, she came face-to-face with Dane.

"Problems?"

"Oh, Lord. Dane, I know it looks bad, but we'll clean it up, I promise. The boys were having so much fun, and the shed did need—"

"You have paint on your nose."

His expression was benign, his tone of voice bland. Not knowing what to make of it, Stevi stared at him blankly. "What?"

"Paint. Here." He touched his right index finger to the tip of her nose. "Hmm. Dry. So's this and this." One by one he touched her forehead, cheek and chin.

No wonder she itched, she groaned inwardly; she probably had as much paint on her as the boys did. But more important at the moment was that Dane wasn't snapping her head off. "Aren't you angry?"

Instead of answering, he stepped around her. "Hi, guys."

"Hi, Uncle Dane!" the boys cried in unison.

He ruffled each head of hair, earning himself paint-stained fingers. "Trying to paint your sneakers, Joey?"

"I had an accident." He glanced up at Dane from beneath the same delicate cinnamon-brown lashes his mother had. "Are I in trouble?"

"Seeing it's an accident, that wouldn't be quite fair, would it?"

The youngster shook his head, his eyes wide and somber. "Stevi's gonna get me out."

"I don't know, you're getting to be a big boy; you're probably too heavy for her. Why don't I pick you up and we'll let some of the paint drip back into the can. Then Stevi can unwind that hose over there and we'll see how much of the rest we can wash off you."

Joey glanced at Stevi to assure himself that he had both adults' approval. She gave him an encouraging smile and a nod, but her thoughts were hardly as confident.

What was this all about? And *Uncle* Dane? Even Sweet didn't get called uncle. She watched as he moved behind Joey and easily lifted the boy up, the muscles exposed by his black tank top barely flexing from the exertion. Helpless to stop them, memories of the day he kissed her flooded her mind, and she remembered the way it felt to have those powerful arms locked around her.

"Stevi?"

"Yes?" She gave herself a mental shake and discovered Dane watching her. It was clear by the intimate look in his eyes that he knew exactly what she was thinking!

"Honey, I could use that hose now."

"Right." Embarrassment made her feel awkward, but she managed to get the hose unwound and turned on.

Together, they succeeded in getting quite a bit of the paint off Joey, although it was a good thing Jolene had dressed them in playclothes because his jeans and sneakers were going to retain a slightly white cast. Dane then retrieved dog shampoo from the shed and delegated the boys to fill the large, galvanized tub leaning against the wall by the water faucet and give Bear a much-needed bath. The German shepherd, a glutton for attention, hopped into the tub before it was a third full, and squealing with delight, the boys went to work on him.

After a few moments of watching them, Stevi picked up her brush and the bucket of paint, ready to climb the ladder and finish what Joey had started. Dane stopped her before she had a foot on the first rung.

"I can do that. You take care of the part you were working on."

"You don't have to—"

"I want to."

And *she* wanted him to leave, or at least to explain. But it was clear, as he removed pail and brush from her hands and climbed the ladder in her stead, that he had no intention of doing either. Not knowing what else to do, Stevi picked up Sean's brush, which was slightly less messy than Joey's, and went back to work, too.

It was shortly past noon when they finished. After cleaning up, the boys began to jump up and down excitedly, asking if they were going to go out in the boat now and fish.

"First we eat lunch," Stevi told them.

"What boat?" Dane asked her.

"That one," she said, pointing to the rowboat near the dock. When she saw his eyebrows draw together, she held up her hand. "Yes, I located life preservers for us."

"Well, you're still not going out in that thing. There's a leak and you'd be bailing out water between casts."

"Sweet didn't say anything about there being a leak in it when I asked him if I could use it."

"That's because he never uses it himself."

"But I promised the boys." She sighed, glancing down to see their dirty faces full of anxiety.

"Fine. We'll take my boat."

She didn't bother turning around to look to where he nodded. She was fully aware of the sleek, metallic blue and silver motorboat tied at the end of the dock, just as she was aware of the inclusive "we" he'd used.

"Boys—" She glanced down at her two charges, who were now half wild with glee over the prospect of going out in the more luxurious boat. Little Benedict Arnolds, she thought grimly. "Why don't you go on up and wash, then get the plate of sandwiches and some Cokes from the refrigerator. Sean, you'll find the chips on the counter. I'll be up as soon as Dane and I talk."

"You're not gonna argue, are you? Whenever Mom and our dad were gonna fight, she'd either send us to our room or outside to play."

Stevi had to swallow hard to dislodge the lump that rose suddenly and unexpectedly to her throat. "No, sweetheart, we're not going to argue. Go on. I'll be right up."

"Nice kids," Dane murmured, watching them race each other across the lawn with Bear running playfully beside them.

"They seem particularly fond of you."

"When Jolene decided it was healthier for both her and the boys to leave Butch, I lent her the money for the down payment on the trailer."

"Sir Dane to the rescue. I should have guessed. Is that what this is all about? Did you think I couldn't manage the boys on my own, so you came out to keep a closer eye on us?"

"No." His dark eyes warmed with tenderness. "From what I saw through my kitchen window, you were doing great. I think you'd be a wonderful mother yourself."

He had no right, she thought, dropping her own eyes in defense. He had no right to suddenly decide to be nice to her. Things were hard enough as it was. "What's going on, Dane? I'm beginning to think I'm losing my mind. One minute you're kind, the next you're hostile to the point I think you can't stand the sight of me. I ask you to let me go and you threaten to hunt me down. What do you *want*?"

"I want to apologize. I didn't know where to begin, or if you would even believe me, so I thought maybe actions *would* speak louder than words and I came down to try to show you." He searched her face, saw her inner turmoil, and hurried on. "You have every right to doubt me; for the last two and a half weeks I *have* been acting like some kind of Jekyll-Hyde character. There's no excuse, of course, but the reason was that I was fighting my own inner demon. My pride was stung."

"Dane, I realize how impossibly wrong I was."

"Wait. Let me finish. I need to." He took a deep breath, wondering how one small woman could reduce him to a mass of nerves when coming up against a six-inch knife in a rough seaport bar had rarely fazed him. "I've come to a decision: from now on the doors stay open, and that refers to the one on my side of the duplex as well as the symbolic one that's keeping you here. It's the only way I can think of to show you that I understand: if I want you to trust me, you have to feel that I trust you. That's why I'm leaving the way open for you to fly off, and I'm hoping that it will convince you it feels just as right to stay. Maybe even more so."

Stevi shook her head, regret eloquent in her eyes. "You insist on thinking there's going to be something between us."

"There already is."

She closed her eyes. "All right. Yes, I know it."

"Thank you for at least giving me that." Reaching out, he touched her cheek.

"You're making this so hard for me."

"I can see that, but it had to be said. There's just one more thing, and then I promise to drop it. When the time is right for you and you decide you want to talk about—well, whatever, I'm here." He drew in a deep breath and flashed her an almost natural smile. "Now, about this boat situation. Can I take you and the boys out in mine or not? I *do* know where all the big fish are hiding."

Equally intent on lightening the mood between them, Stevi pretended to give that serious consideration while rubbing at the paint on the tip of her nose. "Maybe I should warn you that the boys are expecting a fish fry tonight."

"Piece of cake." Sobering, he stretched out his hand. "Friends again?"

After only the slightest hesitation Stevi gave him hers. "Friends. Only, Dane—please don't expect too much from me. I can't make any promises."

It took a lot for him to summon a reassuring nod when every impulse in him was keyed to taking her in his arms and proving to her that she couldn't mean that. "I told you, the doors are open."

"Stevi!"

They both turned to see Joey sticking his head around the screen door of her apartment.

"Bear stole the bag of potato chips and he won't give them back!"

"Coming! Why do I get the feeling there's some serious vacuuming in my immediate future?" She shot Dane an oblique look. "I'd better go."

"Sure. Uh, what time?"

"An hour?"

"Fine."

She took one step backward, then another, wondering how a full-grown man managed the same look of winsome appeal that made it impossible for her to get annoyed at Sean or Joey. "If you'd like to join us, there's plenty. Nothing fancy, just chicken salad and bologna sandwiches."

"I have another bag of chips at my place."

Stevi nodded, tongue in cheek. "I suppose that means yes?"

He broke into a lazy lope, passing her in two strides. "Last one in has to clean tonight's catch," he called over his shoulder.

* * *

"Why can't I keep the turtle, Uncle Dane?" Sean grumbled. "It's all I've caught so far."

"I'm tired of the fish eating my bait. I wanna go swimming," Joey mumbled.

Dane paused in trying to get Sean's fishing hook out of the turtle's mouth with his pliers and glanced over at Stevi, who was stretched out on one of the side benches soaking up the sun. Though her eyes appeared to be closed beneath the wide brim of the red baseball cap she'd found in one of the storage compartments, he had his suspicions.

"You can't keep him, Sean, because he's a snapper, and Joey, I thought we'd try one more spot to use up the rest of our bait. Okay? Ow!"

"Stevi! The turtle wounded Uncle Dane!" Joey cried, scooting up beside her on the bench and out of the way of the ill-humored turtle that now had the run of the bottom of the boat.

Stevi sat up and hugged the little boy closer while grinning at Dane over his head. "Poor Uncle Dane. Should I get out the first-aid kit?"

Tossing the pliers back into his tackle box, Dane picked up the turtle by its shell and dropped it over the side. "Keep it up, Miss James, and you could be joining our carnivorous friend. Unless . . . You want to kiss it and make it better?"

She eyed the index finger that even from across the boat carried the scent of their bait. Wrinkling her nose, she slumped down in her seat again. "No, thanks. I'll stick to being the official fish cleaner."

"Don't think there's gonna be any fish," Joey sighed.

"We can always have a good old hamburger and hot-dog cookout," Dane said, planning how he could spend the rest of the day with them.

"Yeah! I like hamburgers better, anyway," Sean said, tossing the bait he had yet to replace on his hook into the water. "So let's go swimming!"

The place Dane chose was a secluded inlet with a clean beach and crystal-clear water. After anchoring approximately twenty feet offshore, he lowered a ladder over the side for Joey while Sean held his nose and jumped in.

"Going in?" Dane asked Stevi as she sat down on the side and dangled her legs in the water.

"Does it look like I'm wearing a bathing suit?"

It didn't require intense scrutiny to make a judgment call, but Dane enjoyed the opportunity to let his gaze drift over her, since up until now he'd had to do that covertly. The white halter top and red jogging shorts she'd changed into before they left were definitely not what he had in mind, but he decided to forgo the suggestion on the tip of his tongue that she hop in anyway. His imagination was doing a good enough job of visualizing what she would look like soaking wet, and he didn't need the strain on his resolve to take things slowly.

Stripping off his tank top and emptying the pockets of his cutoffs just in case, he lowered himself beside her. "No wonder the fish aren't biting," he murmured, moving his own legs through the water. "This stuff's too warm."

"Excuses, excuses."

In retaliation he scooped up a handful of water and splashed it over her thighs. Despite its warmth, her skin was hotter from the sun and Stevi yelped, catching the boys' attention.

"Throw her in, Uncle Dane!"

"Yeah, come on, Stevi!"

As Dane pretended to give the idea serious consideration, Stevi caught his wrists to stop him. "If I go in, you go in," she promised.

Laughing softly, he shook his head. "Threaten me with something I *don't* want, honey."

The laughter in both their eyes gave way to something far more private and intense, something Stevi felt to the very tips of her breasts. It lasted only seconds, but when she released his wrists, she did so as if she'd been scorched.

"It happens so quickly with you," she whispered without thinking.

Sweet heaven, Dane thought, feeling his own desire lance through him. Her honesty alone was going to bring him to his knees. He dragged in a deep breath while searching for the gentlest way to ask the question that had been tormenting him for weeks now.

"Stevi—are you a virgin?"

She shot a quick look at the boys, but they were near the shore busily tying their life preservers together to make a long raft. "That's a strange question to come from the man who told me I should be used to having men make passes at me."

"The Stevi James who sits at my piano every night and croons about the right kind of love with the wrong kind of man, and who makes one forget what day it is when he looks into her eyes, isn't the same woman who kissed me holding nothing back, as if she didn't understand how quickly she could make me burn."

Miserably embarrassed, she drew her cap lower over her eyes. "Don't be shy; say what's on your mind."

"It's nothing to be ashamed of if you are."

"Words of wisdom from a man who probably can't even remember his first time?"

"Unfortunately, I can, though it deserves forgetting; and if you want to lash out at me, push me in the water or take a swing at me, but don't use words, Stevi. Where you're concerned they cut deeper than I think you realize."

He lowered himself into the lake, and with a parting glance at her stunned expression, swam to help the boys who were trying to unravel a sturdy grapevine they wanted to swing from. Stevi watched his powerful arms cut through the water, making short work of the distance he was from shore, and experienced a piercing desire to leap in after him.

He was right. She *had* wanted to lash out at him, and the shameful thing was that they both knew why. In rejecting him, she was rejecting that part of herself they both knew on some level already belonged to him.

When he returned to the boat, she watched Sean glide through the air and drop into the water, not Dane as he climbed up the ladder and grabbed a towel to dry off. She was afraid of what she might see in his eyes.

"Don't brood," he said wearily, sitting down on the bench behind her.

"I am."

"Well, don't. I promised you I wouldn't pressure you, and the least I can do is try to keep my word one day."

"No, I mean I'm answering your question."

"I've already figured that out."

She turned toward him, hugging her knees against her chest. "And?"

"If I'd have known that when that creep in the lounge came after you, I'd have wrung his neck. If it happens again, I will." He raked his hands through his hair, a little surprised at the heat of violence in his voice. "It matters to me, Stevi. Though it shouldn't. I know all the legitimate arguments about what's good for the goose, and double standards, but I'm still glad—and thrilled to know it's me who's made you wonder, me who's touched you in that special way."

"It doesn't change anything," she whispered, her low voice rich with regret. "I won't have an affair with you, and I can't promise to stay."

"Maybe. Maybe not," he murmured, fingering the delicate gold bracelet she wore around her right ankle. "But if you ever do get a notion to leave, how far do you think you're going to get without your heart?"

Chapter Eight

Although Stevi did her best to act naturally around Dane and the boys, his words haunted her the rest of the day. When Sean and Joey decided they'd had enough of playing Tarzan, Dane drove them out to a more open section of the lake to let the children take turns steering, and she managed to join in the fun. Then, as the sun began to slide toward the tops of the cypress trees on the banks and they headed back, she supervised the preparations for the cookout. But all the while she directed and ate and laughed, a large part of her mind was locked in on one thought.

He'd made it startlingly clear for her. No longer did she have to worry about what might happen if she wasn't careful; it already had. The threat was a reality, the fantasy was a fact. While judiciously avoiding any personal involvement with Dane, she had fallen in love with him.

As a young girl, when she'd daydreamed about this moment, she'd seen herself in a garden dressed in a floating chiffon gown that shimmered in the moonlight, dancing in the arms of the man of her dreams. She would tilt back her head, look up into his eyes and the truth would be there between them to be confirmed with a kiss. How wonderful that dream had been. But as she stood at the kitchen sink, rinsing off the last of their dinner dishes, with smudges of ketchup on her clothes—thanks to Joey's bad aim—she placed a hand to her stomach, feeling anything but wonderful.

"Too much sun and excitement?" Dane asked, coming up behind her to drop the forgotten spatula from the grill into the dishpan.

Irrationally she wanted to throw the thing back at him, while another part of her yearned to spin around and beg him to hold her. Instead, she sank her hands back into the soapy water to clean the utensil and murmured a bland agreement.

"Then I'll see that the boys take a quick bath and get into bed."

Before she could respond he was scooping them up from in front of the TV and carrying them off to the bathroom. Stevi watched, struck how this could easily be an image of the future—if only things were different.

Not tonight, she moaned inwardly, leaning an elbow on the edge of the sink and rocking her forehead against the back of her hand. For just one night she needed a break from thinking and planning and worrying, or she was going to shatter into a million pieces. Dropping the spatula, she blotted her hands on the kitchen towel beside her and headed for the front door.

A half an hour later Dane found her sitting on the top step of the deck, leaning back against the railing post. Bear lay beside her, happily gnawing on a soupbone someone from the café had obviously given him. He stepped over the dog and sat down facing her.

"Mission accomplished. They passed out before they finished arguing about who got what side of the spare bed. What are you doing sitting out here in the dark?"

"Thinking. I've just decided that what this deck needs is one of those freestanding swings. A porch isn't complete until it has a swing."

"Is that so? I'll put it on my shopping list."

"I'm serious."

"So am I."

She shook her head, bemused, then closed her eyes and took another deep breath of the sweet, smoky night air. Dane let his gaze wander at will, from her almost serene face to her white halter top. Ketchup stains and all, she was a delight to look at. "You're feeling better."

"I think—I'm coming to terms with some things."

"That's a provocative statement."

"Don't push," she murmured, peering at him from beneath her heavy lashes. "Just let me figure this out for myself, okay?"

"Would you prefer to be alone?"

"No. How's that for being inconsistent?"

"Who cares? You gave me the answer I wanted to hear."

Chuckling softly, she shifted and wrapped her arms around her updrawn knees, her laughter ending on a sigh. "I had a nice time today. Thank you."

"You sound surprised."

"Relieved. I hated things being strained between us."

He wanted to touch her, hold her. But because he knew if he did, he might not be able to let go again, he shifted instead to mimic her position and pressed his forehead to his knees. "Stevi." His voice was a tortured whisper.

"I'm sorry. Who said honesty was the best policy?"

"Don't stop. I'll cope."

"Maybe we should change the subject?"

"Reduced to talking about the weather like two polite strangers."

Understanding the hint of bitterness in his voice, Stevi wanted to alleviate it. She tilted back her head to gaze up at the sky. "Tell me about being on one of those rigs. I was thinking about that just before you came out. I've heard people say the stars appear closer at sea."

"I guess they do. And sometimes you feel as though there's no one out there except you and God."

"That must have been reassuring when a storm blew through."

He shot her a dry smile. "There were a few times when I thought that even He had left for dry ground."

Stevi's shiver was uncontrollable. "I don't think I could stand it, knowing that someone I—cared about was out there at the mercy of something as mercurial as the weather."

"There are other jobs that are a lot more dangerous." But seeing the way her knuckles turned white as she gripped her legs, he added, "I was single, honey. There was no one waiting for me, no one who cared."

Hearing the loneliness in his voice, Stevi turned her head to search his face, thinking of Delia. "Did she break your heart?"

"Not as much as you could."

The silence that followed stretched until it was an interminable gap between them.

He expected—well, he didn't know what he expected. He'd hoped, though, for more than to see her fold up like a hybrid flower against the night air, her hands clasped over her lips, her eyes closed to an emotion he couldn't reach out to understand. Anger heated his blood. Panic turned his skin cold. He wanted to argue, but against what? She was locked inside herself, imprisoned by her own secrets. And he'd promised her patience—hadn't he?

Feeling a decade older than his years, he rose and lightly stroked her hair. "It's getting late and I promised I'd check in with the night managers at the café and motel before I turned in."

"Dane."

In her voice he heard an entreaty for understanding. Unable to turn away from it, he bent and kissed the top of her head—the comforting, sexless kind of kiss he would give a child. "It's all right," he murmured, before continuing down the stairs.

But it wasn't all right. And for hours afterward, Stevi lay in her bed while sleep evaded her, and peace. How had life become so complicated? It seemed the harder she tried to keep it simple, the more difficult it got. All she'd wanted when she'd begun to sing and play the piano was to earn a decent living to support herself and her aunt. Had she craved fame? Had she asked for a fortune? She'd wanted neither. Then when she was alone, she *had* asked for something out of life, but what? Someone to love. A family of her own to fill the empty well her life had become. And just when she was beginning to accept that her future wasn't to be in the town where she'd spent the major part of her life, leaving became a necessity, not a choice, and the dream was abandoned entirely. Timing, she decided—as in a song—timing was everything. If she'd walked away a day earlier, a week . . .

She rolled over to check the small electric clock beside the bed and saw that it was almost three in the morning: late enough to know she wasn't going to get any sleep, and too early to get up. She dropped her face into the pillow, resigned to let the thoughts come as they would.

What was she going to do? She hadn't counted on meeting Dane, hadn't counted on losing her heart to him. She'd tried to resist, asked for space, and when that didn't work, time. He'd given her both and now she was more miserable than ever. He was miserable, as well. He didn't understand. She couldn't explain. It couldn't go on. Her thoughts in turmoil, she struggled with trying to decide what to do.

Tell him.

The truth? Impossible.

Then leave.

Dear God, just the thought made her heart ache and her eyes burn behind her closed lids. It wasn't choices her mind was contemplating but sentences, and although she sought other solutions as she lay there, none came. When the first whippoorwill heralded the promise of dawn, she slipped from her bed, feeling emotionally and physically bruised.

After washing up, she checked on the boys in the other bedroom, grateful to find that at least they had spent a peaceful night and were still deep in sleep. Retying the belt on her short white robe, she moved barefoot and soundlessly from one dark room to another until, in the kitchen, she put on some water for instant coffee.

What to do? The question remained.

On the other side of the kitchen door she heard a cabinet door open and shut, then the sound of running water. Dane was up, too. She stepped to the door and laid her forehead against it.

Tell him, her conscience insisted. *He has a right. You gave him the right when you told him you cared.*

But she knew she could be endangering him in the process.

Aren't you putting him in danger now? Remember the drunk and how Dane came unhesitatingly to help? He would again, and not *knowing might place him in more serious jeopardy. Tell him.*

The water on the stove began to boil. She shut it off and then just stood there doing nothing with it. Her mouth turned dry. Her heart began to pound violently in her chest. She felt a moment of weakness and nausea that almost had her groping for the counter to steady herself. Instead, she stiffened her spine and went to the door.

He hadn't slept; he hadn't touched a drop of liquor, but he still felt as though all seven of Snow White's dwarfs were playing eight ball in his head. He needed the coffee that was not quite ready to perk. He *wanted* Stevi. His life, in a nutshell, had gone to hell.

He leaned back against a counter and pressed his fingertips to his closed eyes, silently cursing the helplessness he felt. What was he supposed to do that he hadn't already done? What was the magic formula to set things right? He'd tried compassion; her independent streak had shut him out. He'd tried threats; the look on her face had equaled his own. Playing a long shot, he was giving her space. He could almost hear his father calling him every variation of a fool.

When you've met that one in a million, you'll know it, son. There isn't another feeling quite like it. She'll make you feel like a king and a little boy at the same time; and with a smile she'll give you the strength to do the work of three men. You let a woman like that slip through your fingers, and it'll haunt you the rest of your days.

But she wasn't slipping; she was walking. And there wasn't a thing he could think of to do about it. And that's why, when he heard the dead bolt on her side of the door turn, he thought it was all wishful thinking.

The door opened soundlessly. It should have creaked, groaned, at least, from the weight of the abusive thoughts he'd flung at it through the night. Then he saw her standing there looking as pale and as lost as he felt.

Did he take the first step or did she? It didn't matter; in two he had her in his arms, crushing her close and vowing to himself that nothing would convince him to let her go.

"I couldn't stand it any longer," she told him, her face buried against his throat, her arms holding him as tightly as he held her.

"I'm glad. I'm so glad." Searching, he found her mouth, claiming it with his own and ending any further chance for apologies or promises. For the moment it didn't matter, anyway. What counted was that she'd stopped fighting him. For a man who had expected nothing, it was a rainbow before sunrise.

The kiss went on and on. It was sweet and warm, unrushed, though beneath there was a power that hinted at restraint. No, he told himself, this wasn't a moment for the fiery passion they'd shared in their first kiss. This was their real beginning; a moment to cherish.

Stevi's breath trickled out in a shaky sigh as Dane moved on in the tender exploration of her ear and neck. She'd never been worshiped before. Even his hands touched her with wonder, his fingertips tracing what his lips had tasted. Closing her own hands around his wrists, she carried one, then the other, to her lips and pressed her own adoring kisses into each palm. She watched surprise and emotion widen and darken his eyes. Then he was drawing her close again, and with one hand splayed deep into her hair, he held her to his pounding heart.

"I was ready to break down that door," he murmured, his lips brushing her forehead. "I didn't know what else to do. You seemed to be slipping away."

"I was only trying to do what I thought was right." Giving in to impulse, she rubbed her cheek against his hair-roughened chest. He hadn't yet put on a shirt or shoes and he only wore a pair of stone-washed jeans. She loved the feel of him. He was so strong and yet so smooth. Sighing, she placed a kiss at the base of his throat. "We have to talk."

"In a minute. Kiss me first." Once again he took her face within his hands and tilted it upward. "Take away a little of the hunger," he whispered against her lips. Then his tongue slid deep, and what had been an entreaty became a claiming.

This time, control slipped slightly for both of them. Need threatened to overwhelm finesse, and Dane had to keep reminding himself that she was untouched in order to bank the desire bubbling like molten lava within him. But, oh, she was precious! he thought, trailing his hands down to her hips to gently urge her closer. And his! It was a vow that went soul-deep within him. No one else would know these kisses of abandon. No one else would know the sweet torture of having her body, clothed in little more than two wisps of seductive cloth, melting against his. His!

Did the word burst from him like steam hissing from a volcano ready to erupt? No—it was the coffee boiling over onto the stove. Dragging a much-needed breath into his lungs, he turned Stevi out of harm's way and reached over to turn the burner off.

"See how quickly you go to my head?" he asked, giving her a wry smile.

"Why did you turn it completely off? It can't be ready yet."

"I don't want it anymore. I have you."

As he began to lower his head again, Stevi touched her fingertips to his lips; her eyes, still luminous with passion, searched his, begging for understanding. "We do need to talk."

She was afraid. He could see it, feel it. "You don't have to," he began, wanting to show her in some way that it didn't affect what was between them. "I love you, Stevi. Nothing you say or do can change that. It's not a choice I made. You gave me none," he mused, tracing the curve of her cheek with the backs of his fingers.

Tears filled her eyes. "I didn't expect the cowboy to be a poet."

"Consider my inspiration."

He was killing her and she closed her eyes to seek the courage to continue. "You hardly know anything about me."

"Teach me." He gently kissed away the teardrop that slipped from her left eye.

"I *lied* to you." She waited until he raised his head. "My name isn't Stevi James, it's Stephanie Dibert. James was my uncle's name—James Claude Dibert."

"I take it you didn't do it for professional reasons?"

"No, and legally my name is still Dibert. If you had asked to see some kind of identification that night I came to your office, you would have discovered that."

"But you knew I probably wouldn't."

"Yes. The turnover rate for waitresses in most places is almost as high as it is for customers. It's too much of a bother for employers to keep good records on them."

"Why tell me now?" Dane asked quietly, his body betraying to her the tension he felt.

It cost her not to lower her gaze from his, but suddenly she was frightened. She wasn't by nature a gambler. "Because of what you said," she whispered. "And because I—I don't want to leave you. You have the right to know the truth *and* the risks."

For a moment Dane considered that. "Are the boys still sleeping soundly?"

"Yes. Jolene told me they're always hard to wake up. Why?"

"Because I have a feeling this is going to take a while." He lifted her into his arms.

"Dane! What— Where are we going?"

"To get comfortable."

He carried her into the living room that, like hers, was in the "efficiency" style, open to the kitchen. The last time she'd been in his home, she hadn't had a chance to do more than briefly note the blue-and-brown color scheme, and this time was no different. Before she knew it, he'd sat down on a long, coffee-brown suede sofa and she was settled across his lap.

"Better?"

The tenderness in his voice and his gaze reassured her. She pressed a kiss to his unshaven cheek. "Yes, but I still don't know where to begin."

"Your name sounds Cajun. Where's your accent from?"

She shrugged. "My aunt's voice lessons helped me enunciate, and neither she nor my mother were Cajun."

"How did you lose your parents?"

"A freak lightning strike. We lived on a small farm and they'd been working a field trying to beat a spring storm. They didn't make it."

"I remember you said you were a baby. Were you in the house at the time?"

"My Aunt Bette was taking care of me. I vaguely remember it because it was the only time I remember seeing my uncle cry." She glanced down at the way Dane had linked his hand with hers. "This isn't really what you want to know."

"Wrong, but I understand the nervousness. Go ahead and jump a few years if you'd like."

Stevi wet her lips. "It was after Uncle Claude died. My aunt was devastated. As much as they fussed at each other when he was alive, she depended on him; he never let her work. But now there were bills to pay. He didn't have any insurance, and what savings there were went for the funeral expenses. She tried to do some custom sewing for a while, but her heart wasn't in it. It soon became clear that if we didn't want to lose the roof over our heads, I was going to have to take over."

"I'm guessing job opportunities were few and far between?" Dane asked, stroking the back of her hand with his thumb.

"We were an insignificant little town about an hour south of Shreveport. I'd been doing some clerical work in the local grocery store while waiting for a position in the bank to open up, but it wasn't enough to support us. I tried to convince my aunt that we needed to move to the city where I could try to get a better job. She wasn't leaving Uncle Claude, though. Then she began having these fainting spells. The doctor said it was her heart; there were office visits every few weeks and medication to buy. That's when I decided to swallow my pride and do something I'd promised myself I'd never do. I went to ask Louis for a job."

"Who's Louis?" Just as quickly as he asked it, something triggered a memory in Dane.

Stevi smiled bitterly and bowed her head. "I thought you'd put it together."

He hadn't yet, but he didn't like the vibes he was getting. "You thought the guy in the lounge was Louis," he said, trying to see her eyes. "You thought Louis had come after you. Why?"

She ducked her head lower, trying not to lose control, but this was bringing it all back so clearly, and she was tormented enough in her dreams.

"Stevi, *why*?"

"To kill me."

Dane hadn't been in a church for longer than he cared to think about, but that didn't mean he didn't have strong spiritual beliefs; still, the word he uttered was sheer blasphemy. Then, ignoring Stevi's shocked look, he caught her against him and tucked her head under his chin. "Give me a second," he muttered, willing his heartbeat to slow down.

Its fierce thundering echoed in her ear. His arms were steel bands across her back. Never having felt safer, she wished the moment would go on and on.

"I had a feeling it was this serious—you didn't seem the type to be given to dramatics—but I didn't want to face the possibility."

"Now you understand why I didn't want to get close to you."

"You were protecting me. That's sweet, songbird." He ducked his head to place a series of soft kisses near her eye, mouth and ear. "But you should know by now that I can take care of myself."

"The last man who said that died trying."

For several seconds they simply looked at each other, until Dane gave her a subtle nod. "Okay, maybe you'd better tell me now."

"Louis LaSater owns the only place in town where you can buy a drink—in almost the whole *parish*," she amended, reluctantly sitting up because she needed the distance to continue. "Which should give you an idea of what kind of control he has down there. He'd heard me play once at the mayor's election party and offered me a job, naming a salary that was even better than what I'd heard some of the waitresses were making in tips. But it still gave me great pleasure to be able to turn him down. His club isn't a dive, mind you, but as I explained before, when you work for Louis, he owns you." Her smile was cold. "Unfortunately, I was soon given the opportunity to regret my big mouth."

"You asked him for a job in order to afford your aunt's medication," Dane said grimly.

"And he made sure I did my share of groveling to teach me a lesson that no one refuses Louis LaSater. But he *did* hire me."

Jealousy, acute and irrepressible, shot through him. "Did he want you, Stevi?"

"What? No." She shuddered at the thought. "Thank God. He's a cold man, Dane. Sometimes I think if Satan took human form..." She shook her head, dismissing the thought. "Anyway, I've been told he has a beautiful Creole mistress in New Orleans where he often travels on business."

"All right," Dane said, only slightly appeased. "Then what happened that made you run, and why do you think he's after you?"

Stevi stood up, the nervous energy inside her needing an outlet and finding it in pacing. "He had the parish sheriff killed. I heard him order it."

"Good God!" Dane half rose from the sofa before dropping back down again. "Wait a minute. South of Shreveport... That rings a bell. There was a story in the paper. The guy's name was Duncan or—"

"Drummond."

"Right. But they classified that as a suicide. Wasn't he despondent over discovering he had cancer?"

"*Skin* cancer, the treatable type...and he'd just been reelected to his third term of office...*and* he and his wife had just moved into their new custom-built home. Does that sound like the type of man who drives out to a remote road and puts a bullet in his head?"

Now Dane wanted his coffee, if only to wash away the bad taste that had risen to his mouth. Murder... And Stevi, who had from the first triggered his protective instincts, was caught in the middle of it. "You said you heard him?"

"It was an accident. I'd gotten my stocking caught on a table as I was going to the piano and I wanted to put some nail polish on it before it became a run." She grimaced at his bemused smile. "Women's universal problem—what can I tell you? But the point is, on my way to the ladies' room I heard voices, an argument in the storage room. It was Louis and Drummond."

"Did you see them?"

"I didn't have to; I knew both their voices as well as my own. Drummond was always hanging around the bar getting his free beers."

Dane watched Stevi run her hands through her already mussed hair, the movement exposing another two inches of smooth thigh. He wanted to go to her and make her forget, and later in the tangled sheets of his bed, talk about the future—their future. But there wasn't going to be one until they got through this. Taking a deep breath, he told her, "Go on."

"Drummond was threatening to bail out of Louis's bookmaking operation—that's Louis's real profession. Everyone knows it. There're even some police in New Orleans who find it pays to look the other way. But Drummond said the state's attorney general was about to crack down on illegal gambling operations and that Louis's was the first name on the list. Louis was furious. He told Drummond that the attorney general's people would arrest a few small fish to pacify the public and the media, and then everything would go back to normal. No one would *dare* arrest him; it would cause a panic in some very high political offices, and wouldn't the public like to know who did business with Louis LaSater? Well, Drummond said his head would be among the first on the chopping block and that Louis had better make it worth his while to keep his mouth shut. Then he left. I had to duck into the ladies' lounge to avoid being seen.

"When I came back out, Louis was still back there, only this time he was talking to one of his men—he always had a few bodyguards hanging around him. He told the guy, 'Our friend Drummond wants us to take care of him. Don't disappoint him.' I should have run right then and there, but I just froze. That's when one of the cocktail waitresses came down the hallway and asked me why I was standing there looking like I'd swallowed a live frog. Naturally Louis heard and came over. I did my best with my stupid panty-hose story, but he knew I was lying. I could see it in his eyes." She stopped in the middle of the room and closed hers, remembering. "The next morning they found Drummond."

Dane rose and went over to her, directing her back into the kitchen. "Come on. I'd better get that coffee finished. I think we could both use some."

While he waited for the coffee to finish, Stevi opened the front door to take a deep breath of fresh morning air. It was light now, though the sun hadn't yet risen, and the birds were making their usual cacophony, though somehow it sounded like an orchestrated symphony to her.

After the coffee began to perk, Dane lowered the flame and crossed over to stand behind Stevi. He wrapped his arms around her waist, and when she relaxed and laid her head back against his shoulder, he brushed his lips against her hair.

"You said there was a man who tried to help you and that he died. Who was he?"

"Paul Anderson, one of the bartenders. He was a nice man. We'd become friends. He could see that Louis was watching me more closely than normally and he insisted on helping me. I shouldn't have let him, but my aunt had only been gone a short time and I was so frightened, so alone.''

"Don't blame yourself for a decision he made, Stevi.''

"It's difficult not to,'' she replied wearily. "You see, he came up with a plan. After work one evening he was going to drive me home as he usually did. But instead of leaving, he would wait for me to pick up the suitcase I was to have ready and he would drive me to Shreveport. From there I was to buy a bus ticket to the farthest place I could afford. But we were only on the road a few minutes when he spotted the car following us. Louis had been on to us all the time. Paul knew he couldn't lose them, so he pulled off onto a heavily wooded side road and let me out. He said I was to take my suitcase and wait in the woods, that he would be back for me as soon as he was certain it was safe.''

Dane felt tension turning her body rigid and knew she was near her limit emotionally. He turned her around and folded her against the warm strength of his own body. "It's all right,'' he murmured, stroking her back. "Take your time.''

"Oh, God. He never made it around the bend. Louis's driver realized he'd been played for a fool and had turned around. Paul apparently tried to accelerate too quickly and he lost control of the car. He went off the road and into a tree. He'd been smoking, and the gas fumes... Oh, Dane!''

He tightened his hold while her tears that had been held in for too long finally sprang free. He felt no impulse to withdraw as many men he knew would when confronted with a weeping woman; rather he found himself experiencing contradictory urges. He wanted to protect, and he wanted to commit violence. There would be a time for the latter, he promised himself, and gave Stevi all the comfort he could.

After a while, she excused herself and went to his bathroom to splash cold water on her face. Dane took the time to pour two mugs of coffee and carried them back to the living room. When she rejoined him, she looked exhausted but calmer.

"Here," he said, handing her one of the mugs as she sat down beside him on the couch. "This will help."

Having sat for a while, the coffee was strong, but Stevi was grateful for that. She felt numb inside, like a punching bag that had taken all the blows it could stand.

"When you're ready, I want you to tell me the rest."

"There's not much more to tell."

He eyed the wobbling mug clutched between her hands, and then her. "Try again."

Warm granite, that's what his voice made her think of. She sipped the hot coffee and drew strength from both.

"I went deeper into the woods and found a shack belonging to an old woman who put me up for the night and drove me to Shreveport the next morning—no questions asked. I got a job and I thought I was safe. I thought I could put it all behind me the way Paul told me to. But I was wrong on both counts.

"When Louis realized I wasn't in Paul's car, he sent people looking for me. One of them found me. I barely got away from him and caught the next bus leaving town. The rest you know."

How well he did. Everything, from the time he played on her conscience to force her into taking Henri's place, to the way he'd ignored all his instincts about her and cut her down for rejecting him. "Why don't you hate me?'' he groaned, putting down his mug to rub both hands over his beard-roughened face.

She didn't pretend not to understand. ''You did what you thought was right at the time, the same way I did.''

He looked at her then and saw the emotions she no longer bothered to hide. She had been through so much and he had put her through more, yet she could still look at him like that. Slowly, he took her mug from her and set it down. Without hesitation she moved into his arms.

''When I think of what could have gone wrong, what could still happen, and the jerk I've been,'' he said, closing his eyes against the terrible pictures his mind formed. ''Never again. I'll never hurt you or risk your safety again. First thing tomorrow morning I'll drive you in to see Lon Bolton. I've mentioned him to you before—he's the parish sheriff. We'll tell him your story. He'll know how to get Drummond's file reopened and contact the attorney general's office. I'll bet LaSater is behind bars within twenty-four hours.''

''And free on bail in under two. I meant what I said, Dane. He's a powerful man.''

''He doesn't own us and he sure as hell doesn't own the attorney general. That's as good odds as any.''

Stevi rocked her forehead against his shoulder. ''I'm so frightened, but I have no right to let you get involved in this.''

''You have *every* right.'' He framed her face within his hands. ''Take it. Take me,'' he whispered, touching his mouth to hers.

He made it so easy; a gentle persuasion. Her lips parted to his and when he leaned back against the sofa's cushions, she glided with him. Legs stretched and tangled; breaths caught at the sensual intimacy.

"I lay in bed all last night—have for weeks now—wanting this," he told her, fascinated by the delicacy of her collarbone, the draping neckline of her robe and gown. As he kissed her again, he slid his hands from her waist to the gentle swells of her breasts.

Stevi stretched under his caress, aware of the inevitable hardening of his body. The wonder, the strange sensation of power it gave her, showed clearly in her eyes.

"How can someone who kisses like you do be such an innocent?" he moaned.

"I've never kissed anyone the way I kiss you."

Desire, hot and piercing, shot through him. Unable to resist it, he clasped a hand to the back of her head and drew her toward him. He wanted what was his. He wanted to fill himself with her, drown in her sweetness. Live with her. Pausing, their lips almost touching, he wanted to say it. Ask. No, demand.

But Stevi was already drawing away, frowning. "Dane, I think I hear—"

"Nothing. Come back here."

"Omigosh!" She sprang to her feet and hastily straightened her clothing. "Jolene and Sweet are here!"

Now he heard Sweet's heavy step on the stairs, too, and Jolene's light laughter. Grumbling things about lousy timing and too much traffic, he got up and followed her to the screen door in the kitchen. "Hey! Over here," he called in a loud whisper over Stevi's head as they both stuck theirs out the door.

"You look like a totem pole," Sweet replied, ushering Jolene across the deck.

She nudged him with her elbow, picking up on things much faster. "Are we interfering with anything? I know we're early, but we were so excited we wanted to get back here and share it with you.''

"We've been up talking all night," Sweet said, his grin widening as he took in Dane's unshaven face and Stevi's attire.

Dane lifted his fist in mock warning and drawled, "I hear there's a lot of that going around."

"The boys are still sleeping. We were having coffee. Want some?" Without waiting for a reply Stevi went to the cabinets to get two more mugs, then realized she didn't know where Dane kept them. "Oh."

Everyone broke into laughter. It was a perfect summation of their situations. Giving her a quick hug, Dane retrieved the mugs for her.

"Sweet, they're talking to each other again," Jolene whispered. "Isn't that wonderful?"

He glanced at Dane's beard again and then took in Stevi's slightly swollen lips. "I don't know that much talking's been going on...."

"Don't tease. You know payback can be murder." She turned to Stevi and grasped her hands. "Oh, this makes it perfect. We were worried how we were going to approach you."

"Approach us for what?"

"Goose," Dane murmured, squeezing her shoulders lightly. "Can't you guess? They're going to get married."

Stevi uttered a cry of delight and hugged the glowing woman before her, while Dane extended his hand to his friend. For a few moments there were four conversations going on at once.

"Wait a minute," Stevi said, waving her hands. "I'm not following any of this. Are you serious? Mr. and Ms.

Shyness of Bayou Landing are going to have the short-est courtship on record?''

"Unless you two beat us to it," Sweet drawled, winking at Dane.

"Well, we *did* know each other for nearly six months, if you count the time I spent working at the café," Jolene murmured shyly.

"We can't," her fiancé grumbled. "You didn't say a dozen words to me in all that time, and six of those were 'Hi' and 'Bye.'" But he kissed the top of her curly head and shrugged to the others. "It just seems right, you know? Once we started talking we couldn't stop, and soon it was all out on the table. She knew how I felt, I knew how she felt."

"We decided why wait."

"We're getting married next Sunday."

"We want you to be maid of honor and best man."

Stevi slumped back against Dane and glanced up at him. "Are you getting as dizzy from following this as I am?"

"Sounds like a day for major announcements."

Understanding only too well what he meant, Stevi shot him a pleading look before pushing Jolene and Sweet toward the connecting door to her side of the house. "Why don't you go and see the boys. With all this noise I'll bet they're waking up. Then we can all have breakfast together."

"Downstairs," Dane added, catching on. "I'm not cooking pancakes for Sweet. He's a bottomless pit."

When they were alone again, Stevi turned in Dane's arms and wrapped hers around his neck. "Dane—"

"Don't even ask it."

"A week, that's all I'm asking for."

"It's been put off long enough."

"But they're getting married!"

"And you're living under a threat on your life." He tightened his right arm around her waist and sank his left hand into her hair to tilt her head back farther. "Ask me for anything else, *anything*. But not that."

"I want them to be happy."

"I want you alive."

She went on tiptoe and pressed her lips to his. "A week. What's a week? And I'll be here where you can keep an eye on me all the time. Please?"

As her brief, nibbling kisses became less coaxing and more ardent, Dane felt his resolve go up in flames. "Damn it, Stevi. All right. But first thing next Monday morning we're going to see Lon."

"Thank you."

He crushed his mouth to hers, praying he wasn't making a grave mistake.

Chapter Nine

I'd elope."

Stevi grinned at Marge in the vanity mirror of the ladies' lounge. She was coming around, she decided. Yesterday the older woman had still been offering to buy Jolene an hour on an analyst's couch. By Sunday she would wager no one's handkerchief would be more tearstained than Marge's.

"Have you found a dress to wear yet?" Stevi asked, thinking of the powder-blue one she'd bought yesterday on a quick excursion to Texarkana with Jolene. It was simple, really—an off-the-shoulder T-shirt dress with a wide skirt—but she and Jolene had both loved it. And so would Dane.

"I'm thinking of wearing my black shroud."

"Sounds elegant."

Marge shook her head in disgust. "You're as bad as she is. The way you and Dane have been making calf eyes at each other for the past couple of days, I'm surprised you don't make it a double wedding.''

"And make you miss out on another chance to wear the shroud? No way." With a parting wave, Stevi picked up her purse and left.

Outside in the darker hallway her smiled wilted somewhat. A double wedding—it was a lovely thought, but an illogical one for her and Dane at this point. Not that she wasn't aware it was on his mind. She had only to look at him to see possessiveness flare in those intense eyes. Still, her future was hazy at best, and as much as she adored him for taking the position he was—vowing to stick by her—she wasn't about to force any permanent ties with him. He didn't have to know about it unless the time presented itself, but she couldn't think of a greater gift she could offer him than his freedom to walk away.

He was waiting for her at the bar, wearing the same black shirt he'd worn the night they met. When she touched his shoulder, he immediately lifted her hand to his lips. As each day rushed by—too quickly and yet not quickly enough—the tender caresses were becoming a necessity between them.

"Sweet wanted to pour you a wine, but I told him to wait in case you preferred something else. Champagne, maybe?"

"Not funny." Dane and Sweet had snuck a bottle of champagne into the café on Monday and mixed it with their orange juice, and she'd fallen asleep while making reception plans with Jolene. "How about a plain soda with a twist?" she asked Sweet when he came over.

He reached under the counter for a glass and dipped it into the ice bin. "Has Dane told you our news yet?"

"If it's about not going on a honeymoon, I don't want to hear it. Jolene's already explained about the boys' having school and her mother working days, but I told her I'd be happy to fill in on the in-between hours.''

''We'll wait and take the boys to Disney World next spring.''

Stevi leaned closer to Dane. ''Are you going to explain to him that honeymoons are for adults, or should I?''

''I'd rather hear more on your ideas of what makes a good honeymoon.''

She cleared her throat and took a sip of her drink. ''Okay, what news?'' she asked Sweet.

''I'm selling him my interest in the lounge and café, and he's selling me his interest in the motel, and Jolene and I are going to build a house over by the side where we'll put in a marina.''

''Well... You two *have* been busy.'' She glanced at Dane to see what he really thought of the idea. ''You're going to have to look for a new bartender, I suppose.''

''And a new waitress. Sweet will want Jolene to have the chance to stay home with the children while they're young. Before you know it I'll have to, um, step up my search for another piano player, too.''

Stevi was grateful her complexion didn't lend itself to blushes. Nevertheless, she was glad Sweet was called across to the other side of the bar. ''Don't be in such a hurry to make plans,'' she entreated quietly. ''They're more in a position to make them than we are.''

''I don't think I like the way you said that. Is anything wrong?'' He looked around the room, his eyes immediately harder. ''Did you see someone you recognize?''

Stevi curled her right hand around his left, a little stunned and humbled to know the depth of protectiveness she could incite in him. ''*Now* who's getting paranoid?'' she murmured, reminding him of the way he gently rebuked her for trying to keep him uninvolved.

He backed off with a smile. ''Wedding jitters.''

''They're for the groom.''

''I'm the best man. Think of the responsibility weighing on my shoulders if I don't get him to the church on time.''

''Wild horses and Miss Dolly couldn't keep Sweet from his date with the minister, come Sunday.''

He gripped her hand a little more tightly, hoping she could see the love shining in his eyes.

Sunday arrived for the patient and the impatient. Stevi, despite Dane's objections, spent the night with Jolene at her trailer, and thirty minutes before Jolene's uncle was due to pick them up to drive them to the church they were crawling on all fours, trying to find Joey's other dress shoe.

''Jolene, it's my guess he's telling you he *hates* the darn things and he wants to wear his sneakers,'' Stevi said, fanning her face. ''Let him.''

''But he promised me he'd look *nice* for this.''

''I've never seen a cuter penguin in my life,'' Stevi insisted, eyeing the little boy in his dress suit who was looking back at her through guilty eyes. ''Now get into the bathroom and take those rollers out of your hair before you have to walk down the aisle with them.''

Thirty-five miraculous minutes later the bridal party climbed into Jolene's uncle's Chevy. Joey was still wearing his high-tops and Sean had a fruit-punch stain on the front of his shirt that his mother hadn't noticed yet—she was too busy putting a last coat of nail polish on her nails.

''You look lovely.'' Stevi sighed, finally taking the polish from her and putting it away in her own purse.

Jolene surveyed her new eyelet-lace dress, which they'd found in a Western store, of all places. The camisole top was cut off the shoulder like Stevi's and the flared skirt was given more fullness by several layers of ruffle-edged petticoats.

"You don't think it's too white, do you?" Jolene ventured.

"No, it's more of a cream color," Stevi assured her.

"Oh, I wish I'd never invited the whole congregation to stay after the regular service for this, but it was the only way I could get my minister and the organist to do the ceremony on a Sunday. Sweet's so nervous around strangers."

"He'll be looking at you. He won't notice anything or anyone else."

Jolene gave her a teary smile. "You've been so good to me. I—oh! I almost forgot." Giving a last blow to her fingernails, she reached into her purse and took out a small package wrapped in floral paper that matched the pink baby roses in Stevi's bouquet. "This is for you."

Touched, Stevi couldn't think of anything to say and quickly opened the small box. Inside was a gold heart locket on a delicate chain.

"I'm hoping it'll bring you good luck," Jolene whispered shyly. "I want you to be as happy as I am."

Teary eyed, the two women hugged each other until Jolene's uncle announced they were a half mile away from the church and maybe they ought to pull themselves together or all those people who thought they were staying for a wedding might get the feeling it had turned into a wake. They separated, laughing, and Stevi put on her new necklace while Jolene worked frantically to repair her smudged eyeliner.

"Stevi, have you got any more tissues in your purse?" Marge asked, tossing the last of hers into the wastebasket under the vanity counter.

She replaced her lipstick in her purse and took out the small package she'd packed just in case. "You're a real rock, Marge."

"Don't rub it in. I'm telling everyone I'm allergic to flowers." Someone else walked into the ladies' lounge and she sneezed for effect.

"You're not going to do that to the flowers on the wedding cake Penny baked, are you?" Stevi teased.

"Very funny. Oh, wasn't it the best wedding you've ever been to?"

Stevi nodded, although the truth was it was the *only* wedding she'd ever been to. Still, she'd been moved by the music and the minister's warm recitation of the wedding vows. But most of all she'd loved walking down the aisle and seeing Dane standing there looking impossibly handsome in his gray suit, his eyes focused on no one and nothing but her. It was a moment out of a fairy tale and one she was sure she would remember for the rest of her life.

Excusing herself, she went to go find the man who monopolized her thoughts. It wasn't easy; O'Neal's was packed and now she understood why Dane had moved all the tables and chairs back into the storage room after closing last night. It seemed everyone wanted to dance to the lively country-and-western band playing on the stereo.

"I was beginning to think you'd snuck out on me."

Stevi covered the strong arms that wrapped around her waist with her own and leaned back against Dane's solid chest. "Haven't you heard? My running days are over."

"Sounds like you met someone worth taking a few risks for," he murmured, turning her to face him.

"There's no use denying it, I'm crazy about him."

"Good. It's only fair, since he's crazy about you." He placed her arms around his neck. "Dance with me. I've been aching to hold you since I watched you walk down that church aisle."

"Wasn't it a lovely ceremony?"

"*You* were lovely...*are* lovely. I had the strongest urge to shove Sweet out of the way and tell him we were trading places with him."

"It's a good thing you didn't," she drawled, aware of the rush of excitement that coursed through her. "He'd probably have shoved you back."

No doubt, Dane thought, glancing across the room to where his friend danced with his new bride. In all the years they'd known each other he'd never seen Sweet in a tie, let alone a suit. "What do you think of his haircut?"

"I still can't believe he did it. And who could he have found on such short notice?"

"Our quiet mouse, Penny—after you and Jolene left last night."

"Oh, I wish I'd been there." She, too, glanced across the room. "They're going to be good together. And I heard Joey ask Sweet right after the ceremony if that meant he could call him Dad now."

Dane felt a stab of envy and silently wished his own future—his *and* Stevi's—was more certain. Just as quickly, he pushed it away. No one's future was ever certain. The only thing a person could do was make sure he damn well appreciated every moment he had.

"Enough about them," he said, nuzzling closer and dragging her scent deep into his lungs. "Tell me about the perfume you're wearing. I'm going to buy you a gallon of it.''

''Then you'll be happy to hear eau de bubble is available at Gramp's grocery at a dollar-nineteen a jug.'' She chuckled at his bewildered look. ''It's the boys' bubble bath. Great stuff.''

He had no doubt. He still wanted to buy her a gallon—and watch her use it. ''Maybe more than education is wasted on the young,'' he whispered, nipping her ear.

''Okay, you two,'' Sweet grumbled, laying a heavy hand on Dane's shoulder. ''Cut it out. The photographer wants to take pictures of us cutting the wedding cake and we want you in them with us.''

''Then we're going to throw the bouquet and garter and skedaddle,'' Jolene added. ''Not that I can imagine either of you being interested in those.''

Dane tucked Stevi's arm through his. ''Lead on, Mrs. Sweet. I need all the good-luck charms I can get.''

The celebrating went on for hours, even after the bride and groom slipped away, leaving Joey and Sean in the care of Jolene's mother for the night. Just when Dane was beginning to have second thoughts about having made the magnanimous gesture of inviting everyone to stay and enjoy, people began to leave. Marge, Penny and Stevi took that as a sign to start cleaning up.

''Forget it,'' Dane said, urging the two older women toward the front door with the rest of the stragglers. ''Tomorrow's soon enough to tackle this.'' He caught Stevi's quick look and nodded his head decisively. ''There'll be time.''

Unaware of the intimate exchange, Marge assured him she and Penny would be back in the morning to lend them a hand. A few minutes later, laden with Penny's mountain of Tupperware, they, too, left.

Silence settled. Dane and Stevi glanced at each other across the room and exchanged whimsical smiles. Slipping out of his jacket and loosening his tie, he went over to the stereo. A few seconds later slow, seductive jazz flowed from the speakers around the room. Duke Ellington. Stevi abandoned the length of crepe paper she'd been toying with and waited for him to cross over to her.

"Finally," he murmured, easing her into his arms. Just as gently, he coaxed her into following the languid swaying of his own body.

"I can't believe it's over."

"Depends on how you look at things. Some would call this the beginning." He touched his cheek to hers. "Tired?"

"No. But I'm expecting my body to point it out to my head at any minute. Jolene and I were up most of the night talking."

"So were Sweet and I. I still missed you, though. It's become a nice habit to have you come padding through that door in the mornings and pouring yourself a cup of coffee."

"I think what you like is getting the extra half hour to read the paper while I cook breakfast."

"I confess, I have a disgustingly large capacity for the domestic, but if it chafes your feminist instincts, I'll be happy to make breakfast tomorrow and *you* can read the paper."

She closed her eyes a little more tightly. "I don't want to think about tomorrow."

He hadn't wanted to remind her, but the realist in him knew that morning would come regardless. He wanted it to. Without clearing up the past, what hope did they have for a future together? Still, he wasn't unaware of the edge in his own nerves.

"Let's get some fresh air."

He turned off the stereo and all the lights except the neon beer sign over the bar while Stevi collected her purse and bouquet. Outside, she waited while he locked up.

"I'm glad I gave Jolene her bouquet back after I caught it," she mused, lifting her own to her nose. "She looked heartbroken at even the thought of parting with it."

"I wish Sweet had decided to keep her garter; if that guy who snatched it out of my hands had tried to slip it any higher on your leg, I was going to ram it down his throat!"

"He was so conscious of your eyes boring into his back, I could feel his hands shaking."

Dane flipped his jacket over one shoulder, and while waving across the street at Jesse, uttered through tight lips, "Let's change the subject, shall we?"

Chuckling, Stevi waved, too. "Okay... I thought it was sweet of you to make sure Jesse came to the wedding and reception... and to close the café for most of the day so the others could come, too."

"I thought it was pretty terrific of you to sing that old Billie Holiday number he'd asked you about."

As they passed under the breezeway heading toward the back, he slipped his arm around her waist. She laid her head against his shoulder. Sunset cast an amber glow on their surroundings and mellowed the mood between them.

"This is the way the place looked the first time I saw it," Dane murmured, stopping her beneath one of the pine trees to gaze out over the lake.

"No wonder you stayed."

"It got into my blood fast," he admitted. "But not as fast as you did."

She raised her hand to his cheek, showing him with a touch and a look what mere words could not convey. She had lost touch with the romantic side of herself over the past few years, and she had her doubts whether love could do all those wondrous things promised in the songs she sang. But if there was a man who could make her believe, make her want to take the chance, it was this man.

Tenderly sliding her hand to his lips, Dane pressed a warm kiss into her palm. "I love your eyes. The first time I looked into them, I felt like somebody'd dropped the floor out from beneath me."

"The first time I saw you I wanted to run."

He smiled. "I remember. Were you that intimidated?"

"No. Attracted, and it terrified me."

Feeling an all-too-familiar heat curl deep in his belly, Dane dragged a deep breath into his lungs. "I had to ask."

He'd been trying to keep his hands off her all week and it was taking its toll on him. The open-door policy hadn't made things any easier; seeing her walk around in her brief robe or shorts reminded him of needs long denied. But it wasn't simply physical gratification he wanted and needed from Stevi; he was looking for something far more complicated and long-term, and he wasn't about to make any mistakes in achieving that.

"Are you hungry?" he asked abruptly.

"After all those hors d'oeuvres and cake?"

He made a comical face and turned her toward the house. "I'm a meat-and-potatoes guy, honey. How do you feel about a grilled steak, salad and a baked potato?"

"Maybe I can keep you company with the salad, but forget the rest for me." They both entered the house through her door since it was the closest. "Why don't I go change, then I'll lend you a hand."

It was on the tip of his tongue to ask her not to choose the pink-and-white striped terry romper she seemed to prefer. The thing was indisputably modest, but it also made her look sweet and soft and left him aching to curl up with her for more than cuddling. In the end, however, he held his peace and when, ten minutes later, she walked into his kitchen wearing the romper, he told himself that at his age he damn well could and would keep his act straight for a while longer.

Stevi's mood was pronouncedly cheerful and he knew it was her way of trying to stop thinking about tomorrow. As a result, when she asked him to tell her about some of his escapades with Sweet, he did them both a favor and rambled off one after the other.

"I can picture you in a—what did you say those headpieces were called? *Ghotras*, right—in a *ghotra*, riding a camel across the desert like Lawrence of Arabia," Stevi mused, an hour later as she toyed with her salad. "But I'm glad Sweet put his foot down and refused to ride one. Being in that jeep when you volunteered to check on that remote well probably saved your lives from those bandits."

That and the weapons they were carrying, Dane thought. But there was no reason to tell her; his intention had been to entertain, not terrify. "Here, stop playing with that rabbit food and take a bite of this." He jabbed his fork into a piece of filet from his T-bone and held it across the table to her lips.

Stevi took one look at the red juices dripping from it and firmly shook her head. "The day I turn into a vampire, I'll let you know."

"That's mostly steak sauce."

"Where's Bear when you need him?"

"He gets the bone."

She wrinkled her nose. "I'll eat it—if you'll let me boil you some crayfish next time."

He popped the bite of steak into his own mouth. "Honey, I'm crazy about your people's music, but your affinity for eating things with antennas and bulging eyes is too much for even this globe-trotter."

"But you said you *liked* shrimp."

"Butterflied, breaded and deep-fried."

"Then you might as well be eating fried zucchini."

"That's the idea."

Trying her best not to laugh, Stevi downed the last swallow of wine in her glass. Dane tried to refill it, but she shook her head and carried it and her salad plate to the sink. "Between all those champagne toasts at the reception and now this, I think I've about reached my limit. If you're not careful, I might start singing *you* Billie Holiday torch songs."

Dane carried his own plate to the sink. "I could listen to you sing all night; don't you know that by now?"

Soapsuds multiplied in the sink. The shadows in the room lengthened, widened and merged, spreading darkness. But Stevi didn't notice anything except the man standing before her. He filled her heart the way he filled her vision—totally.

"What?" he demanded, his fingers tightening on the plate.

"I—"

The phone rang and Bear arrived at the screen door with an impatient bark. Dane muttered something indecipherable under his breath and bent to drop his leftovers into the animal's dish.

"Catch that, will you, sweetheart? I'll take care of the hound."

Shutting off the water first, Stevi answered the phone on the third ring. Balancing the receiver between her ear and shoulder, she picked up Dane's plate and lowered it into the suds.

"Who is it?" Dane whispered as he came up behind her. Unable to resist, he lowered his head and ran a series of kisses along the exposed side of her neck.

"Dane!" The phone began to slip and Stevi grabbed it with one soapy hand. "No one," she said breathlessly, stretching to hang up. "Probably a wrong number. But it could have been someone at the café or motel, and wouldn't *you* be embarrassed!"

"Nope."

"Oh, you." Scooping up a handful of suds, she turned and planted them on his nose. But her giggles soon turned to a scream of surprise as he lifted her onto the counter, and growling like a bear, began to rub his face against the front of her terry romper. "*Dane*...that tickles!"

"Ow!" he muttered a few seconds later. "Those damn buttons are rough on my nose."

Her laughter trickled to a soft chuckle and she smoothed back the hair she'd grasped. "Serves you right." Even so, as she picked up the dish towel and began wiping away the remaining suds from his face, her touch was gentle.

Dane forgot his sore nose. He forgot everything except how good it felt to have her touching him not only with her hands but her eyes. When her gaze settled on his mouth, he felt his ever-present desire for her sharpen acutely.

"Go ahead. Do it," he encouraged.

"You probably taste like soap."

"Not for long. In a minute I'll taste like you." His own gaze dropped to her lips and watched them part. "Do it."

They were almost at eye level and she had to tilt her head. Ever so lightly, she touched the tip of her tongue to his lower lip, then drew it gently between her teeth. Beneath her fingers the muscles of his shoulders tensed, the hands at her waist gripped her a little harder. Mischief sparkled in her eyes as she peered at him from beneath her thick lashes.

"Now you know what I feel like when you tease me," she said.

"That good, huh?"

"You're impossible."

"But you like me."

"I love you."

This time his hands almost hurt. "Say that again," he demanded.

"Dane—"

"*Say it.*"

"But I thought you knew."

"I hoped. I *thought*, but you never actually said it until— Oh, baby." Caution and care were abandoned as he covered her mouth with his.

Behind her tightly closed lids Stevi saw a swirling light, and deep inside her everything churned. It was the same way she'd felt that day in the rain, only this time there were no doubts to stop her. She wrapped her arms around his neck and answered passion with passion.

They explored each other eagerly, sating one level of hunger only to find another, deeper one. Urgency melted into sensual revelation. She found the taste of the wine warmer, richer on his tongue. He sought only more sweetness and discovered a well of tantalizing spice.

When they broke the kiss for some badly needed breathing, they simply stared at each other in mutual fascination. Stevi touched her inner thighs, chafed slightly by the rougher seam of Dane's blue jeans. The backs of her fingers brushed against his hair-dusted forearms, sending frissons of excitement through both of them.

He dropped his gaze, then wished he hadn't. He wished his hands were there instead of hers. "Stevi—"

"You didn't hurt me."

Instead of answering, he lifted her into his arms. He covered the distance to the couch through blind instinct; his eyes never left her face. Lowering her there, he immediately pressed her deeper into the couch with the long length of his body.

"I need to love you a little," he murmured, his voice a gruff whisper. But his hands were gentle, gentle and reassuring as they slid into her hair and tilted her head to receive the reward of his mouth on hers.

Her eyes fluttered closed as she gave a sigh of ecstasy. In her most private dream she'd fantasized this: what it would be like to be carried off by the man of her dreams to someplace dark and private, to know the power and joy of his possession, to belong, and to become one.

Dane felt her go boneless and fluid beneath his hands; he raced his lips over her face and down her throat as if it would be possible to capture her before she escaped through his fingers. The buttons of her romper were only a slight barrier, and then the journey continued. Beneath his nimble fingers, terry cloth parted. He discovered, as he'd surmised, she wore no bra, but nothing could prepare him for the treasure he uncovered. She was precious and perfect, and he was almost afraid to touch her.

"My hands or my mouth?" he whispered, as she moved restlessly beneath him.

"Both. Everything."

Such cool skin and such heat beneath. The thought enchanted, her taste enslaved. Dane drew her deeply into his mouth and nursed the fantasies that had monopolized his nights for weeks. He would go down into the darkness remembering this first time, remembering the sweet honesty with which she offered herself to him, the innocent eagerness with which she explored him. Although every inch of him burned to quench the fire roaring in him, he would find the patience to wait until he knew the time was right.

With a muffled groan, Dane shifted onto his side and drew Stevi hard against him. It hurt. Not since he'd had a drill bit break and go into his hand had anything hurt half as much.

Unnerved by his fierce hold, Stevi made a tentative effort to ease away. "Dane?"

"Hold me, Stevi. Just hold me for a minute."

Hearing the torment in his voice, she did. Passion mellowed instantly into compassion. But why? she wondered. What had she done wrong?

He could almost hear her thoughts and uttered an angry oath. "It's not you," he insisted, tilting her face up to his. "At least not in the way you think."

"I don't know what to think. I thought you wanted me."

His laugh was short and harsh. "Honey, we're as close as a man and a woman can get without completing the act. Can you not know that I want you?" He kissed her quickly and hard, then drew away slightly to start rebuttoning her clothes.

"Then why? You know that I love you."

"Exactly. You love me, and because you do you were willing to give me the greatest gift in your possession. If you can love me that much, then I can love you enough to wait."

"Wait for what?"

"Lots of things," he murmured, stroking her hair. "A ring on your finger, a trip to the courthouse for a license, you walking down a church aisle in your white gown. Most of all, a wedding night that's as special as it's supposed to be."

"Oh, Dane." Stevi buried her face against his chest. "I wanted this. I wanted tonight because we don't know *what* tomorrow will bring."

"Stop it!" His voice was fierce, his fingers biting as they took hold of her shoulders. "It *is* going to work out for us and you'd better start believing that."

She wanted to. Dear God, she wanted to. She held him tightly and prayed with all her heart.

"I have a favor to ask," she whispered after several minutes.

He pressed a kiss on her damp brow. "Anything— almost."

"Let me sleep in your arms tonight. I can't bear the thought of being alone. Not tonight."

Neither could he. As confident as he'd sounded to her, as hopeful as he was about the future, he wasn't a fool. He could sense trouble, smell it the way you could smell the impending rain. But there was no way he could tell her that.

He simply tucked her closer and placed a tender kiss on her brow. "Then stay with me, love. It's what I want, too."

Chapter Ten

She slept with the trust of a child, and when the ringing phone woke her, she was startled to find it was already dawn and somehow Dane had brought her to his bed last night without having wakened her. As she felt him roll away from her to answer the call, she turned over and lovingly ran her hand down his strong, bare back. They'd slept like two spoons cradled together. She'd never shared that intimacy with anyone else. It had been wonderful. *He* was wonderful.

He caught her hand and raised it to his lips for a brief kiss, but her sleepy smile faded quickly when she both saw and felt his tension in response to something the caller had said. Without hesitation she returned the tightening grip with which he held her hand.

"*What?* When?" He released Stevi's hand to rake his through his hair. "Why didn't you call me last night?"

Frowning, Stevi sat up. Something was definitely wrong. Surely it couldn't be Jolene and Sweet?

Dane glanced down at his bare wrist, then remembered he'd removed his watch so he wouldn't scratch Stevi during the night. He snatched it off the nightstand and did some quick calculating. "Easy, honey— you know I'm coming. Let's see, it'll take me a while to get to the airport, but the shuttles run regularly on weekdays.... I should be in Dallas by eleven."

Stevi listened to Dane's side of the brief argument that followed about taxis. The caller was apparently insisting on meeting his flight. *Honey?* No, no, she thought, rejecting the flash of jealousy that rushed through her. It was obvious someone was hurt; this was no time to be petty.

Even as Dane hung up, he was moving toward the bathroom. "That was Delia. There's been an accident. Clay's been hurt. They've moved him to a Dallas hospital for more tests. I have to take a shower and—"

He stopped in the doorway of the bathroom and spun around. Stevi sat there watching him, her indigo blue eyes trusting, bewildered. She looked adorable, sleep tousled; and he felt like the world's greatest traitor.

Provoked by his silence, she scooted out of the opposite side of the bed. "I can make the coffee and fix you something quick to eat."

Before she could get to the door, he caught her and spun her into his arms. "How can I leave you when I promised?" he groaned, burying his face in her hair.

"He's your brother."

"You're my life."

Closing her eyes at the surge of joy that raced through her, Stevi pressed her lips against his throat. "You make me feel so ashamed. Once I heard you say Delia's name, I didn't want you to go."

"Believe me, if it wasn't for Clay, I wouldn't."

"I know." Stevi kissed him again and pushed him toward the bathroom. "Now, go on and get ready."

In her own rooms she quickly washed up and changed into jeans and a cropped pink T-shirt, then hurried to Dane's kitchen to make coffee and breakfast as she'd promised. She hoped his brother would be all right, but she couldn't help thinking that this might be an opportunity for him and Dane to see that their differences meant little in the face of adversity.

"You know, you never did say what happened," she said a few minutes later when he came into the kitchen.

"Yeah, I realized that myself in the shower. And I'll tell you something really crazy: Delia didn't say. Of course, she always was one to talk ninety miles an hour and leave out half the story, but you'd think she'd at least get it together this time."

"Well, she obviously *was* upset." She eyed the duffel bag he set by the wall, then turned away to get his coffee. "Have a seat. Breakfast's almost ready."

But Dane had intercepted the look. Watching her fill his mug, he caught her hand before she began to move away. "Stevi, the bag's just a precaution in case I need to stay overnight. We don't know how bad this is."

"Of course. It's only— I'll miss you."

"And I'll be worrying about you every minute until I'm back."

"Don't." She returned to the stove, scooped his eggs and sausage links onto a platter, and carried it to the table. "I'll stay out of trouble by cleaning up the lounge, and you know I'll have Marge and Penny to keep me company."

"The lounge." He grimaced. "I forgot. I hate to dump that on you."

"You're dumping it on *us*," she quipped, attempting to tease him a bit. "But if it'll make you feel any better, I'll tell the girls lunch is on you."

"It's a deal."

After that, Dane literally gulped down his food. All too soon Stevi was walking him to his truck. Wearing dress jeans and a tailored white shirt, she thought he looked fresh and capable—and very sexy. Injured husband or not, Delia was going to have to be wearing blinders not to notice.

"Drive carefully," she whispered as he hugged her one last time.

"I promise you we'll go see Lon right after I get back." He glanced over her head, eyeing the diners sitting by the window of the café. "Would it embarrass you too much to be kissed in front of an audience?"

Stevi smiled, her heart in her eyes. "What audience? All I can see is you."

Framing her face between his hands, Dane covered her mouth with his for a long, melting kiss. "That's to remind you who you belong to," he said gruffly when he found his voice again.

She couldn't even form the words to ask him how she could possibly forget. Then it was too late. He was gone. She stood there in the parking lot and watched until she couldn't see or hear his truck any longer.

Finally deciding it was time she got back upstairs to clean up before Marge and Penny arrived, she turned toward the breezeway. It was impossible to miss Chloe standing beside one of the window booths unabashedly grinning at her while she took a customer's order. Stevi gave her back a wry smile and glanced at the man in the booth. At least *he* tried to be a little discreet, she mused, watching him hastily drop his gaze to the menu in his hands. He'd better stay away from cholesterol; his flushed face made her bet he was a prime coronary candidate.

Although they had to work busily in the lounge, the morning dragged for Stevi. Marge and Penny were sympathetic when she told them Dane's news, but she balked at their offer to handle the clean-up detail by themselves. What was she supposed to do to make the time pass except sit by the phone and bite her nails? she asked them. No, she was content with the way they'd delegated things: Penny kept loading and unloading the dishwasher, and Marge and Stevi handled the vacuuming, restoring the tables and chairs to their original places and giving them a good polish.

It was well past noon when they'd finished. Penny had to decline the luncheon offer; she had to take her mother to the doctor. But Marge announced she'd worked up an appetite that would do serious damage to a roasted half chicken.

When they arrived next door, the lunch crowd was beginning to thin out and Chloe pointed them to one of the recently cleared booths by the side window. Groaning, Marge slid into one seat and promptly ordered a straw long enough to reach the iced-tea machine.

"Make that two," Stevi said with a sigh, accepting the menu Chloe handed her.

"Fix you right up. By the way, where'd Dane take off to this morning?"

Stevi told her what she knew, adding, "I'm not sure whether he'll be back today or not."

The waitress shook her head in sympathy, but this was quickly followed by a sly smile. "No wonder he took such a long time to say goodbye."

"Chloe?" Marge asked with saccharine sweetness. "You want me to go get the tea myself?" The smile lasted only until the other woman strutted off. "Busy-body. Did Dane really lay a good one on you?"

"*Now* who's snooping?"

"Never mind. I only have to look at your face to get my answer. I can't remember the last time something embarrassed me. There's another sign of old age."

Stevi shook her head, amused. "You're a real advo-cate for your generation, Marge."

"The day I look in the mirror and find Jane Fonda staring back at me is the day I'll become a cheerleader. In the meantime, I agree with Bette Davis: getting older stinks."

"Jane Fonda works at keeping her figure," Stevi re-minded her.

"Which is why I'm not holding my breath for any transformation—and I'm *definitely* not investing in any new mirrors. God, I'm glad we're closed tonight. When I get home, I'm going to go horizontal on the couch and do nothing but watch the soaps and game shows for the rest of the day."

"Stevi," Chloe said, arriving with their tea. "Sweet's on the phone by the cash register. I told him about Dane's brother and he wants to talk to you."

Stevi gave the ebullient waitress her order and hur-ried over to take the call. As she expected, Sweet gave her the third degree all over again—although she was sure Chloe had repeated *her* conversation with him word for word. Despite her insistence that Dane wouldn't want him to come in the day after his wed-ding, Sweet said he would check with her later to see how she was doing.

It was as she was hanging up that Stevi happened to glance at a man standing at the pay phones a few feet away. The only reason she found herself staring at him was that he was the same man who'd been watching her with Chloe this morning—there was no way she could forget that peach-colored leisure suit. When Chloe brought them their meals a few minutes later, she made a point of asking about him.

"I can't remember who he said he worked for," the waitress replied, sticking the eraser side of her pencil into her heavily sprayed hair to relieve an itch. "But he's got car problems and he's spending the night here at the motel. Hey, he didn't get fresh or anything, did he?"

"Oh, no. I was just wondering. It's unusual to see someone who's obviously not on vacation hanging around all day, that's all."

Chloe shrugged. "If he keeps tipping the way he has been, he can move in, for all I care."

Stevi summoned a dry smile and told herself to stop being paranoid. But she couldn't resist watching the man a few minutes later as he walked up to his room. His attire certainly didn't indicate wealth or taste, but there was a considerable display of jewelry flashing on his stubby fingers.

However, it was the way he opened the lined draperies of his room's windows a few minutes later that caused a faint shiver to race down her spine. He only parted them an inch or two, the way a person would do if he wanted to observe without being caught at it. Just an inch or two. Somehow that ruined Stevi's appetite.

The image continued to haunt her the rest of the day. She spent most of the time in her duplex waiting, hoping for the phone to ring, wanting desperately to hear Dane's voice. She knew she was driving herself crazy and so, finally, around five, she went down to the lounge to practice for a while. Dane would know to call there if he couldn't reach her at the house, she assured herself.

But even while she played thoughts of the man stayed in the forefront of Stevi's mind. It was because she *knew* him, she decided. But for the life of her, she couldn't remember from where or when. And the answer, she knew, made all the difference in the world.

Sweet walked in a short while later, and despite what she'd told him on the phone, Stevi was glad to see him. Giving up her halfhearted attempts to practice, she joined him at the bar.

"Any news?" he asked.

"None. How are you?"

He gave her a broad grin. "Terrific. I've decided married life agrees with me."

"After one day, huh?" Stevi teased. Her own grin became a frown of confusion as she watched him reaching for a glass and some bottles. "What are you doing?"

"Oh, some guy's just ordered room service and asked if he could get a drink, too. Since I'm here anyway, I thought what the heck. Tell you what, though, this is the first time I've ever made a Kir Royale for a *guy*, at least in *this* place."

Stevi's smile wavered. "What did you say?"

"It's a drink. It's usually ladies in fancy joints who—"

"No, the man who ordered it— Sweet, which man?"

He gave her a bewildered look. "I don't know. The guy's in two twenty-one."

She gripped the edge of the counter and drew her lower lip between her teeth. It wasn't a coincidence. It couldn't be. She closed her eyes and tried to remember.... Yes, of course. She'd been sitting at the bar at Louis's one night when a man had come out of his office, sat down a few seats away and ordered the exact same drink—a man she would otherwise have labeled a beer drinker. Later Paul had come up to her, shaking his head. There was no figuring some people, he'd said. Where did LaSater dig up some of his runners?

Stevi's heart plummeted. "Sweet," she whispered, her voice strained. "I need to ask you a very big favor."

When Dane pulled into his usual slot before the lounge a few minutes later, he was tense, tired and not in the best mood, but the thought of being back with Stevi again helped. Just seeing her lovely face would help put what he'd been through today back into perspective. Nothing mattered to him as much as she did.

Spotting Sweet's truck, he shook his head. Now *that* guy needed a serious lecture on priorities, he told himself, heading for the breezeway.

"Dane!" Sweet came out of the café faster than Dane had seen him move in years. "Man, I'm glad you're back."

"That makes two of us. What are you doing here when you're supposed to be home with your bride?"

"Yeah, you owe me. But skip that for a minute. I'm not even going to ask you how your brother is. Since you're here, I'm going to assume he's all right."

"Oh, yeah. He's definitely all right." Picking up on Sweet's tension, Dane scowled. "What's wrong?"

"It's Stevi, she's upstairs packing. It's got something to do with the guy in two twenty-one, but don't ask me what. All she said was something about a guy named Louis coming and that she had to get lost fast. She wanted to borrow my truck. Dane, she's terrified. How could I say no?"

Even before Sweet finished, Dane was heading for the house. "Call Lon," he ordered his friend. "Tell him I need him here. *Now.* And tell him he'll need some backup, that we're expecting trouble. *Move!*'' Breaking into a run himself, he raced across the grass.

Her door was open. He practically jerked the screen door off its hinges to get through it. The first thing that caught his eye was the suitcase in the middle of the living-room floor, the next was Stevi standing by the kitchen counter. It was obvious she'd been writing a note, but after her choked-off cry she merely stood there staring at him as if she'd conjured him out of her dreams.

It only lasted a second—the hesitation, the fear, the doubt. Then they were rushing into each other's arms and holding tightly. Wild kisses followed, and touches too frantic to be called caresses.

"Can't let you out of my sight for a minute, can I?" Dane muttered, trying to find sanity in the midst of his desperation.

"I would have contacted you. I *would*. But—what are you doing here? Your brother—"

"Is fine. We'll talk about that later. First, tell me about the guy in two twenty-one."

"He's one of Louis's people, a bookie. I only saw him once and I'd never have remembered him except that he ordered the same drink he'd ordered at Louis's bar, a Kir Royale. If you saw him, you'd understand why it stuck in my memory."

"And you think he's recognized you?"

"I'm positive. Louis's people are hustlers. The dust never settles around them unless it's for a purpose. I know he's contacted Louis and has been told to stay put and keep an eye on me until Louis can get here himself." Stevi touched his cheek lovingly. "Dane, I have to get out of here. I don't want anyone else to get hurt because of me."

"No one's going to get hurt. I just told Sweet to call for reinforcements. It isn't exactly the way I'd planned to do this, but it's as good as any other." Then, gazing down at her teary, frightened face, he uttered a groan and hugged her again. "God—do you know what it would have done to me to come back and find you gone? Do you think I would have waited until you contacted me before I went after you?"

When he kissed her, Stevi kissed him back with equal fervor. Didn't he know it would have devastated her to leave? Didn't he understand that it was *because* she loved him that she would have done it?

"How charming."

The quiet, slightly accented voice broke them apart as nothing else could. "Louis," Stevi gasped, her gaze locked only on the man in the center of the three standing just inside her doorway.

"Ma chérie..." He inclined his dark sleek head gallantly. "You never cease to impress me. Not only have you succeeded in leading me on quite a chase, but it would appear you've won yourself yet another champion. How fortunate for me that Tully here was passing through on—well business, and happened to recognize you."

Dane met the other man's look of amusement with unmistakable contempt. No wonder Stevi had gone as pale as death beside him. The man looked about as safe as a cobra, and about as charming. A few years older and shorter than Dane, LaSater wore his obvious wealth with a casual elegance that only those who truly believed they *deserved* it could. The half-unbuttoned white shirt was silk; the black suit, with the jacket draped negligently over his shoulders, would easily pay for his own entire wardrobe, and the shoes were real alligator. But Dane didn't envy the man his trappings.

One look into those black, emotionless eyes and he knew his elegant clothes gave him only a fleeting pleasure—as did anything he wanted and obtained.

"That's right," Dane replied, his voice low but deadly. "She's with me now and we can do this the hard way or the easy way, but whichever, you're about to visit some friends of mine at the county jail."

LaSater glanced at the blunt-faced giant on his left and the silent man reached into his jacket and drew out a gun. "You're the one who doesn't seem to understand, and more's the pity," he said, running his finger along his narrow nose. "After all, it's nothing personal, simply a case of tying up loose ends."

"Oh, God," Stevi whispered.

Dane didn't take his eyes off the man holding the gun but he slowly reached out and moved Stevi behind him. "In about five minutes this place is going to be crawling with police. I don't think you can afford any more blood on your hands, do you?"

"Very chivalrous, but not very imaginative; however, just in case your poker face hides more than a bluff, I suggest we move quietly to the car parked at the back of the motel. "René, if you would encourage our guests..."

The big man began to gesture toward the door with the gun, but before he could, Dane kicked out, striking him in the wrist with the edge of his shoe. The automatic went flying, and the giant grabbed his broken wrist in agony. Not giving him time to recover, Dane gave him a blow to the back of the neck and the man went down like a sack of cement.

At the same moment Bear leaped against the screen door, snarling and barking angrily. The other man with LaSater, the man in the peach-colored suit, flattened himself against the hardwood door in terror.

"Hey, I don't want any part of this. I was only doing what he told me!"

"Shut up, you fool!" LaSater snapped, half turning toward him.

It was a ploy. Dane realized it too late and barely dodged the knife in the Cajun's hand when he swung back at him.

"I don't think you will find me as slow on the reflexes as my unfortunate companion," LaSater said, shrugging off his jacket.

But Bear refused to be ignored. Again and again he beat against the screen and finally it began to give. At the sound of its rip, LaSater glanced over his shoulder.

It was enough. Dane abandoned karate for a clean right hook that sent the man backward through the door. He would have kept moving, possibly falling straight over the railing and breaking his neck, if it weren't for the hold Bear took of his leg.

"Well, hell," muttered Sheriff Lon Bolton, lumbering up the stairs moments later on the tail of his two deputies. "Leave something for the cavalry, pooch."

Hours later, Stevi found herself wondering if any of the strangers filling her living room were ever going to leave. It was almost dark; she was exhausted. She'd told her story to the sheriff, to the deputy who took it down for their reports, to the two state police officers who were called in, and then to the FBI agent who finally showed up. It was clear to her that she would be telling it again to the attorney general and finally to a jury, but it was nothing less than she wanted now—what she needed to do to set things right. However, what she *had* to have right now was a few minutes alone, because all the pressure was beginning to catch up with her.

Beside her, Dane felt her growing tension and fatigue, and wrapped his arm more firmly around her. He hadn't left her side since the sheriff's arrival, except to satisfy himself that LaSater and his men were being taken away in handcuffs.

"Excuse me, gentlemen, but if it's all right with you, I think the rest of this can wait until tomorrow." Though his tone was polite enough, there was no mistaking the look in his dark eyes. The matter was *not* negotiable.

Slowly the room cleared out. The last to leave were Sweet and Jolene, who'd arrived after she dropped the boys off with her mother.

"Now, remember," Jolene said as Sweet led her to the door. "If you need anything, you feel free to call."

"All I want is about ten hours of sleep and a long shower—not necessarily in that order," Stevi said, crossing the room to give her a hug. "But thanks for the offer, and for being such a good friend. This isn't the way I wanted your marriage to start off."

"Are you kidding? Anyone can go on a honeymoon. How many people can say they spent the first day of their marriage participating in a major crime bust?"

"I'm going to get her out of here before she decides she means that," Sweet muttered. Having a second thought, he backed up and planted a quick peck on Stevi's cheek. "That's for doing what you did to make sure we had our wedding. It was pretty neat of you—dumb, but neat."

Chuckling, Stevi watched them go down the steps, coaxing Bear to go along by promising the dog the biggest bone in the café. When she turned back into the room, she saw that Dane was still leaning against the kitchen counter, but he was watching her in a way that almost made her forget her fatigue. She closed and locked the hardwood door and went straight into his arms.

"Oh, I need this," she whispered.

"You were terrific. I'm very proud of you."

"*Me?* You saved my life! Where did you learn to fight like that?"

"Here and there." To silence those kinds of questions he claimed her mouth for a deep kiss. When it was over, she was limp in his arms. "I love you."

"I love you. Oh! Dane, how awful. With all this going on you never told me how your brother is doing. Do you want to call him? How badly was he hurt? Will he be in the hospital long?"

"Whoa," he said, drawing her to the couch where they both sat down. "Clay is fine—at least physically. Emotionally is another story."

"I don't understand."

"No, and I'm not sure I know how to tell you." He stroked his hands up and down her back, touched the soft curls framing her face. She didn't need this on top of what she'd been through tonight, but he couldn't think of any way around it. "To make a long story short, Clay wasn't hurt. Delia made the whole thing up."

"But why?"

"To get me to Dallas where she was hoping to convince me to run away with her. Remember that phone call last night that you thought was a wrong number? It was her. When she heard you answering my phone, she decided she was going to play her hand any way she could."

Stevi shook her head, hardly able to comprehend. "That's horrible—not only to treat Clay that way, but to give you such a fright."

"I could have cheerfully strangled her. Instead I phoned Clay from the airport and told him where h could find his wife, and why. Then I told him I w headed back home to my own fiancée. His lack of s prise at Delia's duplicity leads me to believe he's going to be seeing an attorney to file his own divorce papers in the morning. But enough of that. It's over. It's *all* over." He began to lower his head again but stopped when he saw the pensive look that crossed Stevi's face. "What?"

"Dane, it's not over by a long shot. Do you think LaSater's going to just let this happen to the empire he's created?"

"Give the system a chance this time. He's made too many mistakes. And anyway, if all else fails—which it won't—you know they're going to get him on income-tax evasion. Remember Capone? On second thought forget Capone, forget LaSater. Kiss me."

A long while later Stevi laid her head against Dane's chest and sighed contentedly. "Does this mean I can keep my job?"

"Provided you sign a contract this time," he replied, making some different plans in his own mind. "A *long* contract."

"I'd consider it, provided there were substantial fringe benefits."

"You're looking at him."

Stevi laughed delightedly. "Where do I sign?"

"Right here," Dane whispered, lowering his mouth to hers once again. "Definitely right here."

*   *   *   *   *

Silhouette Special Edition®

NAVY BLUES
Debbie Macomber

Between the devil and the deep blue sea...

At Christmastime, Lieutenant Commander Steve Kyle finds his heart anchored by the past, so he vows to give his ex-wife wide berth. But Carol Kyle is quaffing milk and knitting tiny pastel blankets with a vengeance. She's determined to have a baby, and only one man will do as father-to-be—the only man she's ever loved...her own bullheaded ex-husband!

You met Steve and Carol in NAVY WIFE (Special Edition #494)— you'll cheer for them in NAVY BLUES (Special Edition #518). (And as a bonus for NAVY WIFE fans, newlyweds Rush and Lindy Callaghan reveal a surprise of their own....)

Each book stands alone—together they're Debbie Macomber's most delightful duo to date! Don't miss

**NAVY BLUES
Available in April,
only in *Silhouette Special Edition*.
Having the ''blues'' was never
so much fun!**

SE518-1A

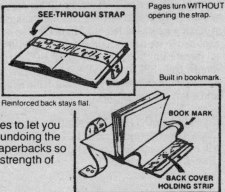